D0527824

RESURRECTION

CITY OF COVENTRY LIBRARIES

WITHDRAWN

FOR SALE

3 8002 02246 618 1

RESURRECTION

GREG KEYES

TITAN BOOKS

Coventry City Council	
APL	
3 8002 02246 618 1	
Askews & Holts	Nov-2015
SF	£7.99

XCOM 2: Resurrection
Print edition ISBN: 9781785651229
E-book edition ISBN: 9781785651236

Published by Titan Books
A division of Titan Publishing Group Ltd
144 Southwark Street, London SE1 0UP

First edition: November 2015
10 9 8 7 6 5 4 3 2 1

This book is a work of fiction. Any references to historical events, real people, or real places are used fictitiously. Other names, characters, places, and events are products of the author's imagination, and any resemblance to actual events or places or persons, living or dead, is entirely coincidental.

Copyright © 2015 Take-Two Interactive Software and its subsidiaries. Take-Two Interactive Software, Inc., 2K, Firaxis Games, XCOM, and their respective logos are trademarks of Take-Two Interactive Software, Inc. All rights reserved. All other marks are property of their respective owners.

No part of this publication may be reproduced, stored in a retrieval system, or transmitted, in any form or by any means without the prior written permission of the publisher, nor be otherwise circulated in any form of binding or cover other than that in which it is published and without a similar condition being imposed on the subsequent purchaser.

A CIP catalogue record for this title is available from the British Library.

Printed and bound by CPI Group (UK) Ltd, Croydon, CR0 4YY

Dedicated to my brother-in-arms,
Charles Lawton Williams.

"OUR SATELLITES CAME down like so many shooting stars," he told Ivan. "What few we managed to get up in the first place. We had no idea what we were dealing with."

"But you tried," Ivan said. "You fought."

He dredged up a rasping, humorless chuckle. "Yes. We fought. And most of us died."

He regarded Ivan critically across the crate that served as his dinner table. The battered lawn chair and three-legged stool he and Ivan were perched on rounded out his wealth in furniture, unless you counted the ragged futon in the clapboard-and-sheet-metal shack behind him.

Ivan seemed very young, very enthusiastic. So much so that at first he worried the fellow was acting, was another collaborator tracking down what little remained of XCOM. But there was something about him that was convincing.

Besides, he didn't have much to lose. If Ivan wasn't

what he seemed—well, he wasn't going to be taken alive. And it would be over.

He took another drink of what he charitably thought of as whiskey. He remembered a time when he had savored a good Highland single malt or American rye. Back then, he would spend half an hour sipping a single shot. Now, he had to make do with whatever rotgut he could find. But then again, these days he only cared about the impact of the drink.

"What do you want from me, son?" he asked.

"There are many like me," Ivan said. "Many with the will to fight the aliens, to win our world back. But we need leaders, men and women who were there. Yes, the aliens beat you, but—"

"The aliens didn't beat us," he snapped, half-surprised at his own sudden anger. Still inside of him, after all these years and a determined campaign to deaden it.

"Sir?"

He took another drink, a long one.

"So you have people willing to fight," he said. "That's great. But you need much more than that. We had it all— an international coalition to fund us, the best scientists and engineers in the world, highly trained soldiers, aircraft, excellent leaders—everything. We shot two of them down; did you know that?"

"No, sir," Ivan said.

"Well, we did. We were making headway on cracking their technology, developing the tools we needed to beat them. Our losses were heavy, yes, but we believed we had a chance. I believed."

"Then . . . what happened?" Ivan asked.

"The coalition caved on us, that's what. Gave us up. I'm not sure which country went first—it's not like they did it to our faces. But in the end they cut us off. The aliens hit our headquarters and major facilities in a coordinated strike. Someone gave them our locations."

"Why?"

"Panic," he grunted, taking another drink. "They were afraid that if we kept fighting, the aliens would exterminate us all."

"Do you think they would have?" Ivan asked.

He snorted. "They could have done that from the beginning. Instead they were conducting small raids, abducting people, spreading fear. I think they got exactly what they were after. A compliant population of sheep."

"I'm no sheep, sir," Ivan said. "My comrades aren't sheep. My father was an XCOM squaddie. He died fighting them in Minsk."

"What was his name, your father?"

"Sasha Fedorov."

"I remember him. He was a good man."

"I didn't know him," Ivan said. "I was still in my mother's womb when he died."

Ivan hesitated for a moment, seeming to sit up straighter in his seat. "Sir, will you help us?"

"Haven't you been listening? We had all of Earth's resources at our fingertips. And we lost. What have you got?"

"Heart, sir. Determination."

"Heart. Determination. That and this bottle of whiskey might be able to get you drunk enough to forget the whole thing. Ninety percent of the human race is perfectly fine with the way things are now. More than fine, from what I can tell. Who are you even fighting for?"

"The abductions haven't stopped, sir," Ivan said. "Thousands go missing every year."

"Right. he said wryly, "And for the most part—you call yourselves 'Natives,' right? You get the blame for that. The people swallow that right along with the rest of ADVENT propaganda and that god-awful stuff they're feeding people now."

"CORE, sir."

"Yeah. CORE. 'Reclaimed protein'. That should raise a few eyebrows. Reclaimed from what? But it doesn't. People eat it. And those weird vegetables . . ." he shook his head.

"There are more of us than you think," Ivan said. "And many more who just need a little hope. You can give them that hope, sir."

"No," he said. "I can't. Because there isn't any. The war ended twenty years ago. More people head into the New Cities every day." He took another swallow. "Now kindly get the hell out of here. I'm bored with this conversation."

"It took me a long time to find you, sir," Ivan said.

"Yes, thanks for that," he said. "It means I have to move again. Go. Leave all of this. I'm not asking again."

Ivan reluctantly stood, and for a moment the young man looked just like his father from almost two decades earlier.

For an instant, something hitched within him, and he remembered how he'd felt back then.

The pride. The purpose.

The Commander.

It was a fuzzy memory, and as he watched Ivan disappear into the Peruvian cloud forest, he began taking larger gulps in the hopes of erasing it entirely.

Part I
Natives

"From what little I've seen of their technology . . .
if the aliens were intent on conquering Earth, there's
not much we could do to stop them. I'm guessing
they have something else in mind."

—DR. RAYMOND SHEN, XCOM CHIEF ENGINEER

CHAPTER 1

AMAR JERKED BACK reflexively as a ferromagnetic slug translated a few cubic centimeters of concrete wall into vapor and white-hot spalls that scattered tiny plumes of smoke on his body armor. He'd gotten a glimpse of her position, though. At least it looked like a "her."

His earphone crackled.

"KB?" It was Thomas, his squad leader.

"Heartbroken, Chief," Amar replied, wiping the sweat trickling down from his unkempt mop of black hair. "I thought she was the one, but she's just like all the others—trying to kill me on the first date. About thirty meters, Chief, and I think another one over your way."

"That's a damn ugly woman if you ask me," piped up another voice. That was Rider, off to his left. "You're better off without her. Kakking jabbers. What're they doing way out here?"

"There are at least six of them," Thomas said. "We need

to roll up this side before they can encircle us."

"I've got you covered, KB," Rider said. Playtime was over.

"Moving up," he said.

Rider's assault rifle started chattering, and Amar slipped from behind the wall, hammering across the kudzu-covered concrete toward a pile of overgrown rubble. He was almost there when Rider's fire stuttered off, and an armored head appeared from the other side of the debris. He yelped and dove, but then Rider fired again. He heard the telltale sound of a bullet striking metal as he squatted.

"Took the bait," Rider said. "Don't know if she's down."

"Took the bait?" Amar yelped indignantly. "I was the bait! You used me for bait!"

"Damn fine bait, too," she replied.

Off to his right, he heard Chitto's shotgun boom once, twice. Then a general conversation of arms began.

Amar took a deep breath, let it out, and jumped up.

The jabber was waiting for him. He heard the whine of the mag rifle firing even as he pulled the trigger. In that very long moment, he saw Rider's shot had glanced from the black, insectile mask, scoring it deeply. He saw the muzzle of the magnetic rifle pulling into line with him and holes appearing in the jabber's armored chest as his weapon spit bullets into it.

Then he was standing there, looking at a dead jabber.

"Jabber" wasn't what they called themselves, of course, or what most people called them. To the majority of people on Earth, they were ADVENT police, peacekeepers, protectors. Supposedly they were citizen volunteers, but Amar had never known anyone who had volunteered. He had never met anyone who knew anyone who had volunteered. And they spoke an odd language amongst themselves that wasn't Hindi or German or Malay or—according to Chitto—Choctaw or any other Earthly language. Which was why Amar and his squad called them jabbers.

As Amar watched, the mag rifle exploded. It wasn't much of an explosion—no danger to him—but the weapon was now useless. They always did that, which was too bad. It would be nice to have one of the damned things. Or better, a few hundred.

"KB?" Rider asked.

"Got her," he said, feeling his pulse beating in his temples. His fingers were starting to tremble. So close . . . "You rang her bell pretty good," he said. "Couldn't draw a bead on me."

"You're welcome," she said.

"Come join the party."

He glanced back quickly and saw her slip over to his right and up.

"I'll just—" she began, then yelped, "*Chips!*"

"Rider? What is it?"

He looked over his shoulder and saw Rider spin to her right. As she fired, a red burst from a mag rifle slammed into her chest. She dropped and rolled behind the remains of a wall, her breath whistling over the radio connection.

"Rider!" Everything seemed to shine with a peculiar golden light. Rider couldn't be shot. She'd never been shot. Not even a scratch, in the three years he had known her. Luckiest person in the squad.

"KB?" Thomas demanded. "What's happening?"

He saw Rider's assailants now, two of them, advancing quickly toward her position.

Thomas's headcount had missed some—not surprising given that these guys had had plenty of time to get in place as they arrived, and that all the kudzu and honeysuckle made things thicker than the jungle he had grown up in.

There were more out ahead of him. If he turned his back to help Rider . . .

He didn't have a choice.

"Falling back, Chief," he said.

He fired at the oncoming troopers as he ran for Rider's position. One looked like the trooper he'd just taken down, clad in mostly black armor with a little red on his mandible. The other was bigger, heavier, a walking shield. It projected a faintly luminous energy field that the smaller trooper took care to remain within.

Amar hit the shield bearer three or four times without apparent effect. Mag rounds jetted past him as he ducked down with Rider.

She was panting heavily, and her eyes were wide. The projectile had pierced her armor, but there was no blood—the heat had cauterized the wound, which looked terribly deep. Her always-pale complexion was now bone white, and sweat plastered stray strands of red-gold hair to her forehead.

"*Verdamme*," she gasped. "That's gonna sting in the morning."

"Just stay down," he said. He peeked over the wall and was greeted by another blast. He shifted and fired again, but they kept coming on. He needed to grab Rider and retreat, find a more defensible spot. . . .

Too late he realized that Rider had staggered to her feet and was trying to flank the shield bearer to get a clear shot at the trooper.

"Rider!" he yelled.

"I'm dead already, KB," she shouted. She took her shot but was drilled by mags once, twice. She and the trooper dropped almost simultaneously.

"So there, son of a bitch," she said. Or at least he thought that's what she said. It was so faint. . . .

No, no, no! She was okay. DeLao could patch her up. He just had to take care of this thing. . . .

Amar emptied his clip into the shield bearer, scrambling back, watching it take aim, knowing he was next and there was nothing he could do about it.

Then it rocked back. Amar saw a neat hole had appeared in its mask before it collapsed.

"Toby?" he gasped.

"Yes," the sniper replied. "You're clear on the right. More bad guys up ahead, though. I've got a captain at one o'clock."

"Thank you," he said. "Rider—"

"I saw," he said. "Busy now."

Amar scrambled over the debris to where Rider had crumpled to the ground.

She wasn't okay, and DeLao was not going to patch her up. There was no longer a soul behind Rider's sapphire eyes.

His throat tightened. Rider had been in the squad when

21

he joined it two years ago. She was sarcastic and funny and profane and sometimes a real pain in the ass. She told wild stories about her youth in Utrecht; she was a terrible singer but insisted on singing anyway. She was fiercely loyal to her friends.

And suddenly she wasn't any of that.

Deal with it later. Or die now.

He ran back up to his previous forward position.

"Chitto," he heard Thomas say. "You're with KB now."

That was bad news. Chitto was as green as they came. This was the first action she had seen, and nothing about her suggested to him that she was up to the job.

"Yes, Chief," Chitto said. He thought he heard a quiver in her voice.

He noticed another jabber trying to move around.

"Oh, no," he whispered, furious. "You most certainly do *not*."

* * *

Amar's chronometer said the skirmish lasted just over an hour, but it felt like twenty by the time the last shots were fired and the squad began cautiously sweeping the area to make certain all of the ADVENT forces were dead. His arms felt like lead, and his knee hurt like hell, though he couldn't remember how he'd banged it.

When Thomas was satisfied, she called them to rest. They had walked into the situation with eight soldiers; now they were seven.

It could have been much worse.

But that didn't make him feel any better about Rider. He kept expecting for her to walk up, clap him on the shoulder, and ask how badly he had soiled himself this time.

Now that he had the opportunity to have a leisurely look around, Amar realized that the rubble they had been fighting in was the bombed-out ruin of some sort of complex. About a fourth of the main structure was still standing, two walls forming a corner and a roof. The guts of the three-storied building were open to the air. All of it was blanketed in a sea of vines and leaves.

The squad had been on its way to Gulf City to raid for supplies when Captain Thomas had heard a faint signal on her radio. It was an SOS, in the current code, and the source of the transmission was nearby, so they had followed it. The signal had abruptly gone quiet just before they came under fire.

"The question is," Thomas said, "whether the signal was legitimate or whether it was sent to lure us here."

Thomas was the real veteran of the group. She'd fought with XCOM back in the day, which he figured probably put her at about forty. She had blunt features and dirty blond hair pulled back into a braid, but she kept a few centimeters of her forehead shaved. She had a burn scar on one cheek and was missing half of her left ear. He had seen her take down a jabber with nothing but a knife.

"If it was a trap," Toby said, a frown on his dark features, "that's pretty bad news. It means they've broken our encryption."

"Well," Thomas said, "why don't we just go see? We don't have that long before dark. I'm guessing the signal came from over there." She gestured at the remains of the building.

He heard DeLao groan. Amar knew why—he didn't feel like taking another step, either.

"Arthritis acting up, old fellow?" Amar said, trying to lighten the mood, as he usually did. But it came out weird and flat, and he wished he hadn't said anything.

* * *

As they moved up to the battered structure, they encountered a few more dead jabbers. Amar prodded one of them and rolled it over, making certain it was dead.

Even in the oppressive heat, he felt frost on his spine.

The trooper's mask had come off—whether she had pulled it off while dying or the force of the explosion that killed her had loosened its fastenings, he couldn't tell. But he could see her face.

The lower part of her face looked human—her lips and cheekbones were familiar enough. Her nose was broad, with very little separation from her forehead, but was still within the realm of human variation. But her ears were oddly flattened against her hairless skull, and there was nothing at all human about her large, silvery eyes. They were set too far apart, almost on the sides of her head, and contained no orbs or pupils.

He felt like he was going to vomit.

For twenty years the aliens had been playing with human DNA. This was one result. Had she begun life as fully human and then been altered?

No one could be sure about that.

* * *

When they reached the ruin and entered the only passable hall, they started finding equally dead humans.

They'd made a stand here, obviously, and given their numbers and those of the enemy dead, they had fought well.

To his relief, Amar didn't recognize any of them. They were armed and armored in the same ragtag fashion as his bunch, at least at first glance, wearing whatever ancient bits of body armor they could find and filling the gaps in their gear with patches of Kevlar, cold hammered sheet metal—whatever was at hand. Most of their weapons were decades old.

But upon closer inspection, these guys looked as if they had new gear. New as in months old instead of twenty years.

Still, it hadn't saved them.

"This one's alive!" DeLao said, kneeling and reversing the Mexico City Red Devils cap that held his frizzy brown hair in check.

The man was sitting, propped against a wall just past a turn in the corridor. He was alive, but only barely so. DeLao already had his medical kit out, but Amar doubted they could do much for the fellow beyond easing his pain.

Thomas knelt next to DeLao.

"What happened here, son?" she asked the soldier. "What's your name?"

He looked up at her with pale gray eyes. His lips moved, but nothing came out.

"Here's another live one," Chitto said. Her voice was quiet—she was always quiet. She had moved farther down the hall—too far, actually. She had a frown on her round face, and her wide lips were pressed tight. To Amar, she looked as if she might lose it at any moment.

They had picked Chitto up in an illegal settlement in a contagion zone just a few days before. The squad had been on another mission but ran across her people being rounded up by ADVENT troopers. After they finished off the jabbers, Chitto had asked if she could volunteer. Thomas said yes, and the plan was to take her to a haven for training. Instead, like a bad dream, trouble kept finding them, drawing them farther and farther from their intended goal.

"Wait for the rest of us, Chitto," Amar said, cautiously moving up to her position. "We have to watch each other's backs. You can't just wander off when I think you're in place."

"Yeah, okay," she said.

Amar looked down at the man she'd found.

The fellow was young and wiry, with narrow, pleasant features, and he was unconscious. He wasn't wearing any armor, and he didn't seem to actually be wounded. The cause of his insensible state was likely the dead ADVENT soldier a few feet away who had been armed with a stun lance, the weapon used to break up crowds and protesters—and to take live prisoners. It looked something like a sabre or a long billy club with a knuckle guard and could deliver a powerful neurological shock.

"Hey, buddy," Amar said, kneeling and patting his cheek.

The man stirred and, with a little more encouragement,

opened his eyes, which were pale blue.

"What's . . . what's going on?" he asked. He had a slight accent that Amar guessed was probably Scottish.

"That's what we're wondering," Thomas said, as she arrived. Dux lumbered back to the rear, while Nishimura padded lithely to the end of the corridor. Even in her armor Nishimura seemed tiny, almost birdlike, but she was as deadly as anyone Amar had ever known—and far more dangerous than most.

"Sergei?" the man said, suddenly trying to sit up.

"If you mean the man down there, he didn't make it," Thomas told him, nodding at the young man DeLao had been working on.

The man closed his eyes and sighed.

"That's unfortunate," he said. "Did anyone else . . ." He looked around at them. Thomas shook her head.

"They're all dead," she said.

He seemed to absorb that for a moment, his lips pressed together hard enough to turn white. His Adam's apple bobbed.

"Who are you guys?" he finally asked.

"We picked up an SOS," Thomas said, instead of answering his question. Her blue-eyed gaze stayed steady on the fellow.

"Yeah, that was me," he told her. "I managed to rig up a spark-gap generator and use the steel beams in the compound as an antenna. It didn't have much range, but more than our short-range units at least. You must have been close." His eyes shifted. "You broke the encryption. You're Natives."

"Holly Thomas," the Chief said. "We're out of Felix, at least for the moment."

Felix was the code name for their base. She waited to see what his reaction would be.

"Felix," Sam said. "Outside of Gulf City. I've heard of you guys. Hacked their propaganda system, right?"

"Well, that was our tinkers," Thomas said. "We're more on the shoot-and-loot end of the business."

"Lucky for me," he said. "You can call me Sam. But I can't tell you my cell. It's classified."

"What are you doing here, Sam?" She gestured at the dead trooper. "What were *they* doing here?"

"I'm an analyst," he said, as if that explained everything. He slowly stood up. "This is an old XCOM facility. Not one of the larger ones. I came here looking for data."

"Data," Thomas repeated, dubiously.

"The central facility was destroyed," he said. "Utterly. Pulverized into dust and then blasted again for good measure. But XCOM wasn't stupid enough to keep all of their eggs in one basket. Or, in this case, data in one mainframe. They had backup servers in a closed network. A private mini-cloud. One of the servers was here. Or rather, beneath here. We had just discovered the way down when the ADVENT attack began."

"How did they find you?" Thomas asked.

"I wish I knew," he said. "Colonel Dixon and the rest— they killed the first bunch, but when it was over, Dixon was dead, and there were only five of us left. By the time I found what we came for, reinforcements had shown up and penned us in. I rigged the radio, and we tried to hold them off for as long as we could. Then it got down to just Sergei and me. The cuss there with the stun lance did me." He nodded at the dead trooper. "Did you guys get him?"

"He was dead when we got here," Thomas said.

"Must have been Sergei, then," Sam said. "You must have shown up in the nick of time." His face fell, and he glanced down the hall at his fallen comrades. "For me, anyway."

"We were ambushed," Amar said, starting to feel angry at Sam without knowing exactly why. "We lost someone."

"I'm sorry about that," Sam said. "But believe me, he didn't die in vain. None of them did."

"She," Amar corrected.

Nobody said anything for a moment. Sam stood there, looking uncomfortable.

"So you found something," Thomas said, breaking the silence.

"Yes," Sam said. "Something amazing. Something that will change everything."

"And what's that?" Thomas asked.

"I can't tell you," he said. "It's classified."

"Classified? Classified by who?" Thomas demanded.

"I can't—"

"Tell me that," she snapped. "Right." She turned away from Sam. "We need to roll, *now*. More reinforcements are probably on the way. Sam, you're coming with us. We'll drop you off at the closest refuge."

"No," Sam said, suddenly more animated. "No! You have to come with *me*! I have to show them what I found, or this really will have all been for nothing. I'll never survive on my own."

"No kidding," DeLao grunted.

Nishimura chuckled at that and pushed a few long, fine strands of black hair back up under the camouflage bandana she wore.

"We already have an assignment," Thomas explained, a bit impatiently.

"This is more important," Sam insisted.

"I have no way of judging that," Thomas shot back.

Sam pursed his lips and nodded.

"Fair enough," he said. "May I have a word with you in private, Captain?"

Thomas paused a minute, then gestured toward the outside of the building. Amar watched them walk out of earshot. They stood there for a moment and then came back.

"We're taking him," Thomas said.

"Why?" DeLao demanded. "What did he say?"

"A name," she replied. "Just a name."

CHAPTER 2

THE SQUAD HAD arrived on the scene in a battered Humvee and an ancient pickup truck. Both vehicles were now smoking wrecks, the first casualties of their encounter with the ADVENT.

The ADVENT soldiers had arrived in a flying transport, but as tempting as it seemed, experience had proven it was a bad idea to try and commandeer one. Their controls did not respond to human hands. On a few occasions, some very clever Natives had gotten around that using sophisticated hacking gear, at which point the vehicles had begun broadcasting a silent alarm and tracking signal, which on one occasion had led to the discovery and destruction of an entire resistance cell. The one instance Amar had ever heard of in which the tracking mechanism was disabled, the vehicle had instantly flared white-hot, vaporizing everyone inside and within ten meters of it. ADVENT weapons and armor were equally useless once separated from their bearers.

So they left the transport alone and double-timed it out of there on foot. Amar tried not to think of Rider lying in the kudzu, cold and alone, but if they stayed long enough to bury her, they would likely need burying themselves. In any case, the ADVENT would return her and the other dead humans to their next of kin using DNA analysis, along with a heaping dose of propaganda concerning what had happened to them. The aliens liked things tidy.

* * *

They alternated between a fast walk and a slow run, following the cracked asphalt of an old state road through what had once been pasture and fields but were now twenty years along toward becoming forest. The aliens had returned much of the world to wilderness, luring most of the population into the New Cities they built on the ruins of the ones they had razed in the conquest.

Vast areas between the population centers were closed to human traffic, and entry into them was forbidden due to something the aliens rather loosely called the *contagion*. Whether it was a disease or some sort of bioagent or nothing of the kind wasn't known to the resistance. Yet, whatever it was, the aliens were scared of it. The road they were on was just inside one of the forbidden areas, and as night fell, Amar felt the presence of the unknown lurking somewhere in the darkness.

When it was finally full night, they slowed to an easier pace. The moon rose, a little more than half full, so they didn't need to use their torches. Night birds called in the distance as frogs and insects provided a chorus.

"KB, right?"

Amar had seen Sam coming up from the corner of his eye, so he wasn't surprised. But he wasn't pleased, either.

"Amar," he corrected. "I'm KB to my friends."

Sam's cheerful expression didn't falter.

"Okay, Amar," he said. "Look, I really am sorry about Rider."

So he had asked someone who had died. That was something at least. But Amar still had a bitter taste in his mouth.

"Yeah," Amar said. "But it was totally worth it, right?"

"I didn't mean to be glib," Sam said. "Dixon, Sergei, those guys with me—they knew what we were doing. They understood the risks and the possible gains. You guys didn't. You were just trying to help someone you didn't know. That was noble. I'm sorry any of you suffered for it."

"Yet you've drafted us to go along with you and still won't tell us why."

"I wish I had the authority," he said. "Thomas understands."

"Yeah," Amar replied.

He hoped Sam would go away, then, but he continued to walk beside him.

"So help me out," Sam said, after a moment. "I didn't know Rider, but I'd like to know who I'm with now. Thomas isn't all that talkative. I was hoping you could fill me in."

"I'm not all that talkative, either," Amar said. "And I'm

not a social director." He instantly regretted it—the fellow seemed sincere enough. And he knew what Rider would have done.

But Sam was finally getting the message and dropping back.

Damn it, Amar thought.

"Well," he said, lifting his chin toward Chitto, only a few meters away. "That's Kathy Chitto, some fresh meat we picked up in—what's that place called, Chitto?"

Chitto turned her broad face toward him. She had what his mother would call a moon-face, with dark, expressive eyes. Her jet black hair was cut short, with bangs in the front. She was on the short side, with broad shoulders.

"Conehatta," she replied.

Sam nodded as he caught back up.

"Right," Amar said. "Just a few days from here. We were headed up to—" He stopped abruptly. They hadn't discussed how much to tell this guy about their own operations.

Sam was studying Chitto's moonlit features.

"Are you a Native American?" he asked.

"I'm a Native," Chitto said. "Like you."

"Sure," Sam said. "But—"

"Choctaw," she said with a sigh. "Okay?"

"Noted," Sam said.

Amar wondered if he had misjudged Chitto. Her reply to Sam was the nearest thing to grit he had seen from her.

Amar pointed ahead. "Tomas DeLao, the guy with the baseball hat and crooked nose—he's from Acapulco. Trained as a physician before he fell in with the resistance. The tall, very dark guy that looks like he has a bowl on his head is Toby Ayele. Born in Israel but grew up mostly in North American shantytowns. Sharpshooter. Stay on his good side, or you'll never hear the bullet. The red-headed ogre next to DeLao is Blake Duckworth, but we just call him Dux, which he likes because it's apparently the Latin word for 'duke.' He won't say where he's from, for some reason. He sounds American, though, maybe Midwestern. The woman on point is Alejandra Nishimura, from one of the settlements outside of New Lima."

"And there's you."

"There's me," Amar allowed. "Mama Tan's little boy."

"So why do they call you KB? What's that?"

"Kampung boy," he replied.

Sam stared at him blankly.

"Kampung is what we call the settlements in Malaysia," Amar explained. "A kampung boy is someone who grew up in a kampung. It can mean salt of the earth—or something like a redneck or a hick, depending on who's saying it."

"Got it," Sam said.

"There was this famous cartoon, years ago—"

He broke off as Nishimura raised her hand to signal a halt, then pointed to cover. Amar ducked into the thorny scrub on the side of the road, double-checking his weapon.

For a long, still moment, Amar didn't hear anything but an owl in the distance and the steady whir of crickets. But then, as the quiet settled, he made out the very faint tinny sound of amplified speech, punctuated by a sort of rushing noise.

After a moment he saw Toby stand, raise his rifle, and put his eye to the scope. Then Thomas and Nishimura appeared beside him. They all gazed off in the same direction as Toby. Thomas gestured for the rest to move up.

The landscape was almost uniformly flat, but here and there small slopes developed, the remnants of natural levees formed by the river's flooding. From that slight elevation, looking beyond the still water of an oxbow lake, Amar saw a line of orange flame. As he watched, a jet of fire appeared and set more trees to burning. A second spume of liquid fire jetted at the other end of the line, and another.

"It's ADVENT," Toby said. "I can make their silhouettes out through my scope."

"Yeah," Dux said. "But what the hell are they burning? And why in the middle of the night?"

"Maybe it's something that only comes out at night," Chitto murmured, more to herself than to the rest of them.

"The contagion?" DeLao whispered.

"Doesn't matter," Thomas said. "That's not our mission. Come on, let's move out."

They continued on, and soon the flames were no longer visible. But the wind shifted and brought with it the scent of burning wood.

And something else. Amar didn't know what it was, but it wasn't like anything he'd ever smelled before.

The night was good cover, but he was glad when the sun came back up.

* * *

Around midday Thomas called a halt next to the remains of a country store that had probably been abandoned twenty years before the invasion. From any distance—and, importantly, from above—it looked like a mound of kudzu vines. Nishimura chopped through the creeping tendrils with the long, wickedly sharp blade that served as both her machete and sword, and they finally had a chance to rest.

"We're about a kilometer from the Greenville settlement," Thomas said. "Amar, Chitto, take an hour's rest. Then I need you to go down and see if it's safe. We need supplies, and we need vehicles."

"We have a contact there?" Amar asked.

"We do," she said. "I haven't been able to get through by radio, but that doesn't necessarily mean anything. Then again, it might, so be careful."

"I don't need to rest," Amar said. "I can go on in."

"Take a nap," Thomas said. "I don't need you all woozy-headed; I need you thinking straight."

He agreed, and using his backpack as a pillow, he fell asleep almost the moment his body came to rest on the rotting wood floor.

* * *

They were on patrol, back on the West Coast, almost a year ago. They were all together, joking, talking nonsense. DeLao was talking about this time a guy he knew set a slap-trap and then ended up tripping it himself that night when he got up to pee. Nishimura countered with a tale about a man who once tried to buy her from her mother for six chickens and some ice.

And then they fell strangely silent.

"This isn't right," Amar said. "Something is missing."

The others didn't reply. They just kept marching silently along.

"Really," Amar said. "There's supposed to another story. Something about rigging up a shoe—"

"It was a kakking boot," Rider said. "I set up a boot to swing down and kick my brother in the face when he opened the door."

"That's it!" he said. "Rider!"

"Who?" Nishimura asked, a puzzled expression on her delicate features.

"Rider," Amar insisted. "You know. She's right back there."

He turned to point, and there she was, her dead eyes looking at nothing, her mouth slightly ajar, gaping holes in her armor . . .

He jerked awake, panting wildly, unsure of where he was.

"Bloody hell," he grunted after a moment. Reluctantly, he lay back down, hoping for some dreamless sleep.

CHAPTER 3

AMAR DID NOT feel refreshed when Chitto woke him. He felt hungover without the benefit of actually having been drunk. But he rose and—casting a longing look at his weapons and armor—started out with her on the road to Greenville.

To most people, the New Cities seemed like a great deal. They were clean and neat, and they came with a whole list of benefits. No one went hungry in the cities. No one died of malaria or the flu or a random staph infection, and even the diseases of old age could be staved off with the advanced gene therapy that the aliens had developed. More people moved to the cities every day.

But the aliens didn't force anyone to move. And there were people who didn't care to move to the cities, who still didn't trust the aliens and their propaganda, who remembered that their planet had been taken by force. The independent, the stubborn, the paranoid; natural outsiders and clannish groups holding to themselves, like Chitto's people. All of these and more chose to live outside of the places the aliens had so carefully prepared.

And the aliens allowed it, so long as they didn't build their towns in forbidden areas. But they did nothing to make life in the settlements easy or pleasant.

Parts of the old town still stood—the courthouse, a church here and there, an old strip mall. But most of the settlement was either recently constructed or had come in on wheels. Trailers and RVs accounted for much of the living space, some solitary, with their own little yards walled off, some formed into compounds. Shacks of sheet metal, chicken wire, bamboo, cinderblocks, and other sundry materials had been marshaled to form mostly simple, but sometimes weirdly complex structures. One house on the outskirts was entirely covered in Mardi Gras beads and small plastic dinosaurs, glued into elaborate but mysterious patterns. Mysterious to Amar, anyway. Another was surrounded by wind chimes made of tire irons and frying pans.

If nothing else, the settlements had personality.

Almost every roof sported solar arrays, so they had power. A sniff of the air, however, proved they weren't doing as well in the sanitation department.

To Amar it felt like home, even though his kampung was thousands of miles away, in a tropical climate, where people spoke different languages. While the details were dissimilar, the feel was the same. Settlement life was settlement life, wherever you were.

And the biggest fact of settlement life was the ADVENT. They appeared suddenly, often for no clear reason. They searched warm bodies and houses. They arrested people who were never seen again. Sometimes weeks would go by without a patrol showing up. Sometimes half a hundred would arrive and stay for two weeks.

Given the number he saw at the moment, it looked like the latter was happening here. Greenville was under full occupation.

"Well," Chitto said, "this doesn't look safe at all."

"Yeah," Amar said. "You want to wait here?"

She seemed to think it over.

"No," she finally said.

"Good," he said. "So if they question us, we've just come from your settlement—what is it again?"

"Conehatta," she said.

"Does that mean something?"

"Yes," she replied. "It means Gray Skunk."

"Izzit? That's kind of a funny name for a town."

She shrugged. "I didn't name it."

"So we're looking for a relative of yours," he said. "From Gray Skunk. Is that plausible?"

"We could be looking for my uncle John," she said. "He disappeared a while back."

"That'll work. Uncle John has a medical condition, and we're going to try to talk him into moving into Gulf City for treatment."

"He won't go," Chitto said.

"That doesn't matter," he said, starting to become impatient with her. "We just need a reason to—" He stopped when he saw the slightest curve of her wide mouth.

"Oh," he said. "You *do* have a sense of humor."

As they wound their way through the mazelike settlement, Amar began to feel naked without his armor and weapons, but they were looking to avoid attention, and humans weren't supposed to go around armed to the teeth—or at all, for that matter. Not unless they were ADVENT.

He tried not to look at the troopers for fear his expression would betray him. The memory of Rider's dead face was a raw wound within him, and he was afraid they might see that. Some of the ADVENT were said to be able to read minds, and although he was skeptical of that, it would be foolish to test that hypothesis at the moment. So he tried to think about kittens and flowers and move along as quickly as wouldn't seem suspicious.

Ahead, a few of the troopers were removing debris that had been placed in front of one of their billboards, which was scrolling images of beautiful, happy people living it up in Gulf City. Meanwhile an old woman was wailing as several jabbers dismantled the wall of old carpet she had erected to hide her chicken coop. Livestock of any sort was now illegal—supposedly something to do with the contagion—but that didn't stop people from trying to keep animals.

They reached their destination, an old Greyhound bus, without incident. Its windows were papered over, and COLD BEER was painted across the length of it in large block letters.

Inside it wasn't as dark as he had imagined it would be; the paper was translucent and of various colors, giving the place a sort of rainbow feel. The few characters hanging out on the stools at the bar, however, didn't have any rainbow connections whatsoever.

He and Chitto settled on two of the mismatched seats. The bartender, a young man with dreadlocks, dark skin, and darker tattoos glanced their way.

"Yeah?" he said.

"I guess I'd like a cold beer," Amar said.

The man didn't say anything, but he went to the single tap and filled a plastic cup. The cup bore streaks and patches of color on it suggesting it had once advertised something, probably a movie for kids. He poured the second beer into a mason jar.

"Who wants the fancy one?" he asked.

Amar pointed at Chitto, whereupon they learned that the "fancy one" was the mason jar.

The beer not only wasn't cold, but Amar wasn't sure it was even beer.

"I love a cold beer," he said. Then he waited to see how the man would respond.

The fellow stared at him for a second.

"That's about all we have right now," he said, nodding vaguely toward the front door. "You see how it is."

"Yeah," Amar said. He glanced at Chitto.

"So we're looking for her Uncle John," he told the man. "I don't guess he's been in here? John Warren."

He didn't know what her uncle's last name actually was, but Warren was their black market contact in Greenville.

"He was here," the man said. "He didn't like the beer."

"Do you know where he went?" Amar asked.

"How are you with directions?" the fellow said. "I don't have anything to write them down on."

"I can remember," Amar assured him.

"These directions are a little . . . redneck. Can you deal with that?"

Amar smiled. "I think so."

He listened carefully and then nodded.

"Thanks," he said.

"Don't forget to pay for the beer," the man said.

"Right." He reached into his pocket and plunked a small package on the counter. The bartender took it and quickly slipped it somewhere Amar couldn't see.

Back outside, the images on the billboard had changed. It now showed dead bodies, and with a growing sense of horror, Amar realized that they were the Natives who had been with Sam. They had been stripped of their armor and dressed in settlement-style clothing. He suddenly understood what was coming and tried to turn away, but it was too late. There was Rider in a faded denim jumper, crumpled among them.

". . . the work of unknown dissidents," the voiceover was saying.

Amar felt a wet sting in the corners of his eyes. The thought of them handling her, making her part of *this*, this lie . . . the indignity of it all . . .

"Let's get out of here," he rasped. "Now."

How he managed to hold it together until they were clear of ADVENT eyes he didn't know, but back in the woods he broke and wept like he hadn't since childhood. Chitto hung back, giving him a little space and making sure they weren't followed. When he thought he was capable of holding a conversation again, he waved her up.

"I think we're okay," she said. "Nobody behind us."

"Yeah. Thanks."

They walked in uncomfortable silence for a few moments, which Chitto uncharacteristically broke.

"Did you understand his directions?" she asked.

He tilted his head yes.

"He said to take a left at old man Renfro's back fence," she said, a little indignantly, "and to go about half a mile to the east of Tallaboga Creek."

"Don't your people give directions that way?" he asked.

"Sure, to people who grew up in the area and know where things like that are. Do you know where old man Renfro's back fence is?"

"No," he said. "It doesn't matter. That was all a smokescreen. Only the numbers were important. Third left, third right, third big tree, half a mile, nine-mile creek, first big pile of tires, and so on."

"Oh," she said. "Coordinates."

So she wasn't stupid. That was good.

"Exactly," he said.

"What did you give him for the beer?" she asked.

"Penicillin," he said. "Worth a lot on the black market."

"You trust him?"

"Trust is all we have," Amar replied. "Some of these guys have fewer scruples than others, but they're all businessmen. If you do bad business, word gets around and eventually you're not in business anymore. And they need us, too, to carry their goods through the more dangerous places or 'liberate supplies' from ADVENT outposts. So do I like that they gouge their own people?

No. But with the aliens running things, it's the only economy the settlements have."

* * *

On foot, it took three days to reach their destination. This time, at least, they didn't walk into an ambush. ADVENT ground transports were quieter than internal combustion vehicles, but they still heard it coming in time to hide in the dense vegetation that crowded up to the road.

"This road only goes one place, so far as I can see," Thomas said. "I don't think it's a coincidence that ADVENT is here. What do you think, KB? Did he set us up?"

"I thought he was honest, Chief," he told Thomas. "If he wanted to turn us in, all he had to do was yell."

"Sure," DeLao said. "But then everyone in town would know where his loyalties lay. How safe would he be after the jabbers were gone?"

Thomas fingered the nub of her left ear, a sign that she was conflicted.

"Amar has pretty good instincts about this sort of thing," she finally said. "With this much ADVENT presence in the area, they may just be busting every illegal settlement they can find, and this place is definitely over the line." She shrugged. "We'll know when we get there."

There wasn't much to the place: part of a ruined corrugated metal building, four shipping containers that had been welded together to form a square, and a few smaller shacks arranged on what had once been a parking lot. Also in sight were two pickups, a minivan, and a pair of ADVENT ground transports. The troopers themselves didn't seem to be in any particular state of readiness. Four were visible, but there were likely more inside.

They were looking at all of this from the relatively dense forest surrounding the clearing.

"Toby, do you see a spot?" Thomas asked.

They were close to the river, and the landscape was flatter than ever. There were plenty of trees, though.

Toby had other ideas.

"Over there," he said, extending his lanky arm. "The bridge."

Amar hadn't spotted it, but now that the sharpshooter pointed it out, he could see the concrete supports. It wasn't the main bridge that crossed the river—that was gone—but rather a smaller one to take the road over swampy ground bordering the river.

"That's about three hundred meters," Thomas said.

"Yeah," Toby said. "That's about what I make it."

"Okay," Thomas said. "Go get in position. I can't spare anyone to watch your back."

"Understood," Toby said. He turned and trotted off through the woods.

"KB, Chitto," Thomas continued, "work your way around to the other side of the clearing, about eleven o'clock. When Toby's first target goes down, we'll lay down fire from here. Nishimura, you're over there at two o'clock. You all know the drill."

"Got it, Chief," Amar said.

Amar had barely settled into position when he heard a metallic thud and saw one of the troopers crumple almost gracefully to the ground. Predictably, the others scrambled for cover. Two ran directly into the rocket Dux launched at them. Two more turned and sprinted straight for him and Chitto, trying to get around behind the containers.

He was waiting for them to come into range when Chitto's shotgun boomed. The troopers, surprised but unhurt, unloaded into the trees. Amar ducked further behind the pine, but the mag rounds punched right through it.

Alamak, he gritted. *Bloody hell!*

He rolled out and opened up on the nearest, but both suddenly broke and ran toward transports. One of them went down like a sack, another victim of Toby's eagle eye, but the other made it and was joined by a couple from the building. One of them had the flattened helmet and red sash of a captain.

The door closed, and the vehicle jerked into motion. A grenade exploded next to it but didn't slow it down.

Amar stared after the retreating transport.

"What?" Chitto said.

"I've never seen them give up so easily," he said.

"Easily? We killed four of them."

"Yeah. And by the way, next time you're ready to give away our positions to the enemy, please wait until they're close enough for that boom stick to actually hurt them, okay?"

She nodded, her round face darkening a little.

They moved up the container house.

Amar kept his weapon aimed at the front door, sure

there had to be some trick in this, but then Nishimura stuck her head out.

"All clear," she said. "But there's someone in here."

CHAPTER 4

SHE WAS YOUNG, probably no more than twenty. Her light brown hair was clipped just below her ears, and she wore a belted yellow smock and dark green pants.

DeLao was already examining her, and Amar hoped she wasn't dead. She didn't look much like a smuggler, and he wondered what she was doing here.

"Gather supplies, quickly," Thomas said. "DeLao, what about her?"

"She's fine," he said. "It looks like they gave her something to make her go night-night."

"Do you think they were abducting her?" Thomas asked.

DeLao shrugged. "I don't think they were escorting her to the prom. I might know more when I finish examining her. What I can tell you—"

"Tell me later, if she's not about to explode or something. We've got to acquire supplies and get out of here before those others set up an ambush or call in an air strike or whatever it is they're up to. I don't trust this situation. Make her comfortable in the van. Amar, she's your charge."

"Right, Chief," he responded, wondering how he had somehow become the point man for rookies and the unconscious.

It took less than half an hour to get the vehicles packed up and on the road. The bridge that had once crossed the river wasn't there anymore. During the invasion, the aliens had blown every bridge they came across to limit ground transportation, and most of them hadn't been rebuilt, because ADVENT was still very much invested in controlling transportation and movement. They likewise destroyed rail systems, although in that case they had replaced some of them with their own trains. If they went south, they would be heading toward Gulf City and probably the other ADVENT vehicle, which wasn't at all in their best interest. According to Sam, southwest was the direction they ultimately wanted to go, but they couldn't until they found a river crossing. There was a rumor that someone was running a ferry over to Helena, and that was north, and so north they went, across miles of more flat delta landscape, through the rusting and rotting remains of towns that had been on the wane even before the aliens declared the area off-limits.

They had been on the road less than an hour when the girl awoke with a scream. She was lying on the backseat behind him, her eyes pitching around the interior of the van.

"Hey," Amar said. "Calm down. You're okay."

She sat up, but her gaze kept shifting, settling briefly on Chitto, DeLao, and Dux, who was driving, before returning to him. He noticed she was feeling the back of her shoulder and wincing.

"What happened?" she asked. She had a deeper voice than he had expected. Throaty. "Where am I?" Her eyes were a really startling green color, like jade.

"We found you at a smugglers' compound," he replied. "You were kind of out of it. Do you remember how you got there?"

Her eyes widened. "Smugglers' compound?" She shook her head. "I don't remember anything like that." She frowned. "You're not smugglers, are you?"

"No," Amar said, although he knew that was not entirely true. Why make things complicated? She needed reassurance.

"So what's the last thing you remember?" he pressed, gently.

"I was in Greenville," she said. "That's a settlement."

"I know," Amar replied. "I've been there."

"I went into this bar—the one in the bus. Do you know it?"

Amar told her he did.

Her eyebrows scrunched together. "Maybe I drank too much," she said. "Or maybe . . ." She suddenly looked horrified. "These smugglers," she said, "do they . . ."

"Traffic in humans?" Amar finished. "No. That doesn't happen, ADVENT propaganda to the contrary."

"Unh-unh," DeLao shot back from the front. "It wasn't about that. Check your left shoulder."

"It hurts," the girl said. She pulled her collar down, revealing a crudely stitched incision.

"My implant," she said, blinking in confusion.

"Implant?" Dux grunted, and then proceeded to swear colorfully for about thirty seconds, his sunburnt face flushing bright red. For Amar, it all suddenly made sense—her haircut, the way she dressed. She was not only clean; she had a flowery scent about her.

This was no settlement girl. She was from one of the New Cities. Not everyone in the cities had identification implants, but to receive gene therapy and advanced medicine, you had to have one.

She had that panicked look again.

"What's your name?" Amar asked, trying to ease her back down.

"Lena," she said absently, still craning her neck to stare at her wound. "Lena Bishop."

"Lena, where are you from?"

"I'm from Gulf City," she said. "I guess you figured that out. Who cut out my implant? Why?"

"The smugglers," Amar said. "They probably thought you were a spy. You . . . sort of were."

"What are you talking about?" she demanded. "I just wanted a drink."

"Yes, but when you have one of those things under your skin, they can track you, maybe even see what you see, hear what you hear. So, in a lot of settlements, when someone comes in from the outside, they don't ask questions. They just cut it out of you."

She looked at them all in horror. "Who are you guys?"

"The good guys," DeLao said.

"DeLao," Dux cut in. "Did you make sure it's really out?"

"Of course," DeLao said. "No lump, and the magnetometer didn't pick up a signature. Ran it over her whole body."

"My whole body?" Lena said.

"Nothing inappropriate," DeLao assured her. "I'm a doctor."

"I think that's enough," Dux snapped. "Finish debriefing her with Thomas."

It was unwise to drive at night, so when twilight came they pulled onto a dirt road and followed it until they found a good campsite. Amar helped establish a perimeter while Chitto sat chatting laconically with Lena. When everything was secure, Thomas called a meeting, reviewing the girl's story—first without her, then with her. There didn't appear to be any inconsistencies.

"What were you doing in a settlement, anyway?" she finally asked Lena. "Ghetto tourism?"

Lena looked around nervously. "I think . . . " she began, checked herself, and then started again. "I think I was looking for you guys."

"And what do you mean by that?" Thomas asked.

"The . . . you know. The resistance."

"Huh," Thomas said.

"That's who you are, right? I mean, you have all of those guns. That's hard to miss. And you're hiding in the woods. You were at a smugglers' compound . . ."

"Never mind us," Thomas said. "Why were you looking for the resistance?"

"To join them. You. To fight ADVENT."

* * *

Amar took the first watch. Lena stayed up with him, which was convenient since she was—in part—what he was watching.

"Where are you from?" she asked. "Not from around here, given your accent."

"What do you mean?" he said. "You have the accent, not me."

He smiled to let her know he was kidding, but she didn't seem to get it, and he realized that he couldn't actually feel a smile on his face. It probably looked more like a grimace.

"Sorry," he said. "Just a little . . ." He gave up. "I'm from a settlement in Malaysia," he finally told her.

"Your English is excellent," she said.

He shrugged. "I've been speaking it since I was a kid, along with Malay, Mandarin, and Tamil."

"Ah," she said. "Just put my big ol' foot in my mouth, huh?"

"No worries," he replied.

"I always do that," she said. "My sister Jules used to say I couldn't talk my way out of . . ." She didn't finish, and her smile vanished. He didn't press. A lot of people joined the resistance because someone they knew had gone missing—with or without explanation. That had been the case with him.

"So tell me about where you're from," she said.

"Well," he said, "it's near a place that used to be called

Kuantan. It's on the ocean, and there are lots of palm trees and monkeys. Not a lot to tell, really."

"But it was a settlement?"

"Oh," he said. "Yes. Not a big place. Picture Greenville with palm trees and monkeys."

She looked down. "I'd rather not remember Greenville, thanks," she said.

"Understandable," he said. "They shouldn't have done that to you."

She closed her eyes and smiled.

"Thanks," she said. She sighed. "I'm tired. What's your name?"

"KB," he told her, after a moment's hesitation. "You can call me KB."

"KB, if I sleep right over here, will you make sure I'm okay? Will you keep me safe?"

"Yeah," he replied. "I can do that. It'll be fine."

She lay down on the bedroll they had commandeered for her back at Warren's depot. In minutes, she was asleep. She was still asleep when Chitto spelled him, and he took his own rest next to her, but a half meter away.

* * *

Amar woke with something cold pushing against the side of his head.

"Don't move, KB," someone whispered. No, not someone—Lena. He cracked his eyelids and saw she had the muzzle of Chitto's shotgun pressed against his temple.

"You're going to get up real slow," she said. "And we're

going to go over to that truck, and you're going to get in and drive."

Wow. He had been stupid, hadn't he? But Chitto was supposed to have been on watch.

"Drive it yourself," he said.

"I would love to do that," Lena replied, "if I had the faintest idea how to drive that ancient tetanus trap. But being civilized, I don't."

"You're going to get yourself killed," Amar warned her. "Really, this isn't a good idea. I don't know what your problem is—"

"Well, you'd know all about that, wouldn't you?" she said. "About people getting killed. About killing them. Get up."

"Trouble, KB?" Chitto asked, mildly.

"Chitto, how the hell did she get your gun?"

"I guess I fell asleep on watch," she replied.

"Shut up," Lena hissed. "If you wake the others, I'll really have nothing to lose. I'll die, but you two will go first."

"But," Chitto said, "I did take all of the shells out before I fell asleep. You know. Just in case someone was pretending to be asleep and waiting for a chance to arm herself."

"You're bluffing," Lena said.

Amar slapped the barrel away from his head and then took hold of it. He scrambled up and pushed the butt against Lena, hard, and she fell back.

He heard the hammer click. Nothing happened.

She had just tried to kill him.

Amar drew his pistol.

"This," he informed her, "is loaded."

Everyone was stirring now, coming over to see what was happening. Lena climbed unsteadily to her feet. She was plainly terrified but trying not to show it, and not doing a very good job.

"Was it you?" she demanded. "The bombing in the Helena settlement? Or another bunch of murderous scumbags?"

"What are you talking about?" DeLao snapped.

"You know damn well what I'm talking about," Lena said. "Eight innocent people died. One of them was my sister."

Amar recalled the billboard in Greenville, Rider dressed in civilian clothing.

"There was no bombing at Helena," he said. "That was propaganda. A lie. The dead they showed were *our* dead. Native dead. Really, do you people believe everything the aliens tell you? When you get your implant, do they take out part of your brain as well?"

"My sister was not one of you," Lena exploded.

"Really?" he asked. "What was she doing in Helena?"

"She . . . she was a doctor. She went to help people, to try to bring them into the city. The ones with cancer and tuberculosis, with diseases nobody has to die of anymore. And you assholes killed her."

"Why would we bomb civilians?" Amar asked. "Human civilians?"

"I don't know," Lena said. "I'm not a sociopath." She stood straighter, a look of defiance on her face. "You people drugged me, kidnapped me, and cut me open, and now you expect me to just swallow any bullshit you toss my way? What now? Are you going to kill me now, in your war on clean water and good healthcare?"

"It's starting to sound real damn tempting," Dux muttered.

"No," Thomas said. "We're going to show you something."

* * *

A flight of ADVENT drones delayed their departure the next morning, so by the time they got started it was already getting hot. Their vehicles didn't have functioning air conditioning—other than open windows—and probably hadn't for decades. Twice they had to stop and clear debris from what remained of the road, and in one place a meandering stream had cut a channel right through the highway, forcing them to spend three hours chopping trees to form a makeshift bridge. It was nearly sundown when they reached the ferry.

If Sam hadn't been with them, Amar doubted they would have ever known the boat was there. It was docked underneath part of the bridge that had once spanned the river, protected from sight by canebrakes and strands of willow that Amar thought must have been deliberately planted as screens. The ferryman lived on his boat, an old barge he had fitted out with a biodiesel engine. He was an older man, knobby and gangly, and as bald as an egg. He had about five days' worth of gray stubble on his face. He regarded them all with a great deal of suspicion until he noticed Sam.

"I remember you," he said. "Cocky young fellar. But these ain't the ones you came with."

"No," Sam allowed, "we had some unexpected trouble."

"I'm sure sorry to hear that," he said. "Big trouble, or little trouble that you walk out of but go a different direction?"

"Big trouble, I'm afraid," Sam said.

"Damn. Can't say how sorry I am. That's rough." He sized the rest of them up.

"Come on over to the lounge," he said.

The lounge was the area around the control cabin, which had been decorated with tiki statues of various sizes, some cut from palm trunks, other made of driftwood and even plastic, the latter dating from a distant age. Island scenes had been painted on the cabin walls, and some wicker chairs surrounded a table.

"I'm Captain Simmons," he told them, as they settled into the chairs. "Y'all want some coffee?"

Amar remembered the last time he'd had coffee. It had been almost two years ago, on the long trip from New Guinea to the southern coast of Mexico, a little settlement named Puerto Arista. It hadn't been that good, and he didn't have high hopes for whatever Captain Simmons had brewed up, especially as it came out in vintage tiki glasses. But he couldn't hide his amazement when he tasted it.

"I know," Simmons said. "Had some guys come through a few weeks ago. This is what they paid me in."

"Nice of you to share it," Sam said. "You never know when someone will come through with something this good again."

"The E.T.s may get me tomorrow, for all I know,"

Simmons said. "Or I might have a good old-fashioned heart attack. I always thought coffee was best shared in company, and being stingy never made a man one whit happier. Relating to that, I've got a stew going, if you're hungry."

"That's very kind," Thomas said. "But the sooner we can cross the river, the better."

"Then you have time," Simmons said. "There have been enough air patrols today I don't fancy crossing until night."

So they relaxed a bit as Captain Simmons went to fool with his stew. Fireflies began to drift up across the river.

The stew wasn't as good as the coffee; it seemed like it had been cooking for days and had a little of everything in it. But it was filling and hot.

"Don't you want some?" Simmons asked Lena.

Amar watched the exchange. She had refused food all day. She had to be starving.

The captain pushed a little bowl of the stuff toward her. Reluctantly, she took it and the proffered spoon.

"Thank you," she said. It was the first word she had spoken since the previous night. She took a tentative bite, then another.

"This is really interesting," Lena said. "How did you get it to taste like this?"

"What do you mean?" Simmons said.

"It just doesn't taste like CORE," she said. "I know they say it's like an empty palate, that you can make it taste like anything at all, but to me there's always this taste on the back of your tongue, and you know what it is. I'm not getting that here."

Everyone stared at her for a few seconds, and then Dux

let out a belly laugh, and everyone else joined in. Lena frowned and her cheeks reddened.

"What are you all laughing at?" she demanded.

"There's no CORE in this, honey," Simmons said. "Some squirrel, and a little rabbit, some mudbugs, and I think a little nutria is still in there. . . ."

Lena stared at her bowl.

"This is animal meat?" she gasped.

"Well, yeah," he replied.

"Oh, god." She dropped the bowl and lurched toward the side of the boat.

"Stay with her, KB," Thomas ordered.

Amar was already on his feet. He didn't think she was faking, but she was not one with whom to take chances. He kept his eyes trained on her as she heaved her guts into the river for fear that she might jump or push him in.

"What is wrong with you people?" she managed, when she was finally done.

"We eat what we can out here," Amar said. "There's no CORE in the settlements. Besides, who even knows what CORE is? 'Reclaimed protein'? Reclaimed from what?"

"It's safe," she said. "It's nutritious. No one has to kill it."

"It's bland," Amar said. "It's boring. And it's what the aliens want us to eat. That's enough to put me off it right there."

She wiped her mouth on her sleeve. "Why?" she asked. "Do you really think things were better before they came? There was war everywhere, and famine, and crime!"

"We still have all that," he said.

"But you chose it! There's no crime in the cities, no hunger."

"Because you're *kept*," he said. "Like a herd of cows. And why do people herd cows?"

"They don't anymore," she said.

"Right," Amar said. "Because cows have been replaced."

She just stared at the water, sweat beaded on her forehead.

"Look," he said. "I don't know if the world was better before they came. But it was *ours*. Our fate was in our own hands."

"Pretty shaky hands, from what I know," she muttered.

"A lot of what you know isn't true," Amar said.

CHAPTER 5

THEY CROSSED IN the dark and debarked their vehicles underneath the other end of the ruined bridge. Helena had an actual resistance outpost, and a radio exchange between the cell captain and Captain Simmons confirmed that there was no active ADVENT presence in the town.

The old town of Helena had been largely destroyed by flooding, and many of the new structures were built on stilts, reminding him even more of home. The night was young, and people were out enjoying the slightly cooler air that sundown brought. Someone was projecting an old movie on the side of a Winnebago, and Amar smelled popcorn. Some kids were playing football in a clearing by the river. Helena seemed a little cleaner than Greenville; the smell of frying fish and hush puppies were enough to overwhelm the stench of sewage.

"Okay," Thomas told Lena. "Start asking."

"What do you mean?" Lena replied.

"There was a bombing here, right?" Thomas said. "People died. You were on your way here for a reason."

"Yes," she said. "I wanted to see it. See where she died. I wanted to try to understand."

"Go to it, then. Amar will see to your safety while I meet with the local Natives. The rest of you—take the night off, but stay on your toes. Keep your earpieces in."

Lena looked around for a bit and then walked over to a stand where two teenagers were selling watermelon juice. It turned out they were expected to have their own cups, and when they didn't Amar had to spring for a pair of plastic tumblers.

"Where are y'all from?" one of them, a girl with uneven, blackened teeth, asked.

"We just came from Greenville," Amar said.

"That's a long way," the boy said. "I've never been that far."

"Why are your teeth like that?" Lena asked.

The girl recoiled. "Ain't too polite, are you?"

"So you came up from Greenville," the boy persisted. "Were you there for the bombing?"

"What?" Lena said her brows arching up.

"Yeah," the boy said. "A bunch of people killed, according to the vid stream. Of course, my daddy says the vid stream ain't worth much. Says a hognose snake knows more about the world than folks that watch that."

"No," Lena said slowly. "The boming was here. My sister was killed in it."

"In Helena?" the boy said. "Weren't no bombing. Hell, what's there to bomb in Helena?"

"But . . ." Lena trailed off, uncertainly. "Did you know a woman named Jules Bishop? Looked a little like me, two years older, with blonde hair?"

"Jules Bishop?" The two looked at each other. "Peculiar woman," the girl said. "From Gulf City. She used to help out at the school, but she ain't been around there for a year or two."

"Where is the school?" Lena demanded.

"It ain't open right now."

"Where?"

* * *

The school overlooked the river, a single-room building surrounded by a porch and mounted on pilings so it stood well above the waterline. There were no lights on, but two men were passing a bottle between them. One was Sam.

"I figured someone would direct you here sooner rather than later," Sam said. "But I wanted you to get here on your own."

The other man was little older than Sam, maybe thirty-five. He had a narrow face set in sorrowful lines. He stood up and stared at Lena.

"God," he said, "you look like just her."

Lena looked back and forth between the two men.

"Okay," she said. "I'm not doing this. For all I know, one of you crossed the river early and set this all up for my benefit. I don't know why you would bother, but I'm not—"

"She was my wife," the man said.

Lena closed her eyes. "I'm. Not. Doing. This."

Amar felt his fuse sputtering up its end. Did Lena think she was the only person in the universe who had lost someone? Who did she think she was?

"Right," he said. "I swam over here and coached the whole town to lie. I'm bloody amazing that way." He swept his arms about. "Helena isn't all that big. Did you see anything that resembled a blast radius? Really, what is wrong with you?"

"We corresponded," Lena erupted. "Don't you think she would mention a husband?"

"No," the man said. "Jules wouldn't. My name is Laurent Gerox. ADVENT has been searching for me for years. Jules wanted to make certain they didn't find me through her. Any communication you had with her was recorded and analyzed—if not before she joined the resistance, then certainly after."

"This is all absurd."

Laurent sighed. He put his hands on his knees. "She liked the little things," he said. "A funny turn of phrase. The color of the sky on a clear morning. Cherries—she really loved cherries."

"Stop it," Lena said.

"Her favorite color was aquamarine, and she was very firm about it—not blue, not turquoise, not teal— aquamarine. If you ended a sentence with a preposition, she would always correct you. She once told me that when you were little, you were afraid that some sort of monster lived under your tub. A sewer snake? No, that wasn't it. Something like that, though."

"Slewer snake," Lena said. Her voice was thick, and

tears had begun slowly tracing down her face. "That's how I said it, and it stuck."

"She was in my detail," Sam said softly. "She died protecting me. We had to leave the bodies, and this is what ADVENT does. It lies. All of the time. About everything."

"Why?" Lena asked softly. "Why?"

"Because," Laurent said, "they have something to hide. Because if people knew what they were really up to, more would rise up against them."

"What are they really up to, then?" Lena asked.

Sam cleared this throat. "That we don't actually know," he said.

"My sister died for that?" she said derisively. "For 'We don't really know?'"

"Yes," Laurent said.

"Then she was an idiot," Lena said. She turned and walked away.

"She'll be okay," Laurent said. "I'll see that she gets back to Gulf City, if that's what she wants."

"Good enough," Amar said. As long as she wasn't his responsibility anymore, he was happy.

* * *

They were still flush with fuel and supplies when they left Helena. Now that they were across the Mississippi, they could turn south toward their as-yet-unnamed destination. Their path carried them deeper into a contagion zone than Amar would have liked, but he didn't see anything out of place. Everything looked very much as it had on the other side of the river. The few aircraft they saw were very high and far away.

That night they parked the trucks inside an old farm building of some sort. Dux and Toby began unpacking, and a few minutes later they were again treated to the big man's impressive vocabulary of obscenities.

Amar trotted over to see what was happening, and there was Lena, looking up at the redhead with a defiant glare in her eyes. She had apparently stowed away on one of the pickups by crawling under the tarp.

Before Dux got too out of hand, Amar took Lena by the elbow and escorted her to the edge of the camp.

"Why?" he demanded. "Laurent said he would take you back to the city. Or you could have stayed there."

"You're not telling me everything," she said. "Until you do, you're stuck with me."

* * *

Thomas put Lena under Chitto's guard and called a meeting, out of earshot of the two. Dux got his opinion out immediately.

"We should leave her here," the big man said.

"It's a long walk back to Helena," Amar felt he should point out.

"That's her problem. She'll be fine if she sticks to the road."

"Sure," Nishimura said, slapping at a mosquito. "If a snake doesn't bite her. Or a cougar. Or whatever the aliens are scared of doesn't get her. Or an ADVENT patrol, for that matter. Leaving her here alone might be a death sentence."

Thomas agreed. "I'm not going to leave her in a contagion zone."

"We can't take her any farther," Sam said. "It's too dangerous."

She turned to Sam. "It's time you told us where we're going."

"It's classified," he began.

"Do not tell me that again," Thomas snapped. "Conditions change. We adapt. That's what you *do* when you're in the field. Obviously your old squad knew where they came from. So now we're your escort. You haven't gotten new orders because it's not possible, right? Are you in contact with your superiors?"

"No," Sam admitted.

"So you adapt," she snapped. "Where the hell are we going?"

He took a deep breath and settled his shoulders. Then, reluctantly, he began to speak.

"There is a base," he said. "Near here. Not just any resistance base. An XCOM base."

To Amar, he might as well have just said they were going to meet Sun Wukong, the Monkey King, or Ravana, lord of the Rakshasa. Or King Arthur. XCOM was a thing from legend—another time, another world, even.

"I don't find that likely," Nishimura said. "After all these years? Where have they been? Why haven't we heard from them?"

"The time wasn't right," Sam said. "The world wasn't ready. But soon . . ."

"The name you mentioned," Thomas said. "You're sure?"

"I am completely certain," Sam replied. "You don't know me that well, but I hate to lie. It almost makes me physically ill to lie."

"So instead you don't tell us anything at all," DeLao complained, pulling off his ball cap and fanning himself with it. "Where is this base? You say it's only about a day away. That puts it somewhere just outside of old Houston — basically jabbertown central."

"It's safe," Sam said. "When we get there, we'll be safe. Then this whole mess will be out of my hands, and you can take your concerns up with someone much more highly placed than me. Okay? But we have to lose Lena."

"Not here," Thomas decided. "Somewhere closer to the coast, where she has a better chance of being found."

"What if she doesn't want to be found?" Amar said. "What if she wants to join up? You let Chitto in pretty easily."

"Chitto isn't a brainwashed New City brat," Dux said. "Who knows what she's got kicking around in that brain can of hers?"

"My point is this," Sam said. "If she goes with us much farther into this, letting her go isn't going to be good enough. Do you understand? I'm serious. This is for her own good."

"She stays with us until we're out of the contagion zone," Thomas said. "There are settlements outside of Houston. We'll leave her at one there." She glared at Dux. "And next time, we'll check the vehicles before we pull out."

* * *

Midmorning the sun shone hot and bright, but in the west it was beginning to darken. The trees along the highway first shivered and then began to sway in sporadic buffets of wind. Rain began, like liquid gold in the sunlight.

"Devil's beating his wife," Chitto murmured. They were in the pickup, and Amar was driving.

"What?" Amar said.

"When it's raining and the sun is still out," Chitto explained, "we say the devil is beating his wife."

Amar thought about that for a second, wondering when he'd had this conversation before. "We used to say the fox is marrying the crow," he said.

"That doesn't make any sense," Chitto opined.

"And yours does?" he retorted. She shrugged.

Then, he remembered. "Rider used to say it was a 'chicken carnival'," he recalled, "which makes even less sense."

"Uh-huh," she replied as the rain began to hammer so hard the ancient wipers could no longer clear it.

"I'm not her, I know," Chitto said, after a moment, "but I will watch your back as best I can."

Amar nodded, feeling his breath tighten. "Thanks," he said, as the wind tried to yank the truck from the road.

"I wonder," Chitto said, "why they don't just call it 'sunny rain.'"

"Oh, yeah," Amar remembered. "*Hujan panas.* Some people back home do call it that."

"See, that makes sense," Chitto said. He nodded his agreement.

But by then it wasn't sunny rain anymore. Clouds darker than soot rolled over them, and thunder began pounding their ears. They were forced to slow to a crawl, the taillights of the minivan ahead of them the only thing Amar could see. Then they stopped entirely for fear of driving into something too deep.

They needn't have bothered—the deep came to them. First, Amar felt a sort of tug. Then the wheel turned in his hand. The yellow water outside was rising very quickly, he saw. Then the truck lifted and turned half around.

"Oh, crap," Chitto said.

It wasn't like sea waves, coming and going. This just kept coming, now horrifyingly quickly. The truck raised completely from the road as water began to gush in from the floorboards and seams of the doors.

Then something hit them—a log, another car, he didn't know, but the truck began flipping over, driver side down. His window shattered, and water poured in as the truck continued to roll.

After that, he only remembered water churning everywhere as he gasped for breath, clawing his way out of the window even as the truck turned again. He couldn't tell up from down anymore. All he could feel was a pull like the strongest riptide he'd ever experienced.

Then his head struck something, and he blacked out.

CHAPTER 6

WHEN HE CAME to, something was hanging onto him from behind. He struggled wildly, in a total panic, as lightning limned everything in white and thunder exploded in the same instant, leaving his ears ringing and a long red stripe on his retinas.

He realized then that it wasn't just ringing in his ears. Someone was talking to him. After a moment, he understood that it was Chitto, and that she was behind him, holding his face up out of the water, not dragging him into it. She was holding onto something else with her other arm.

"Your armor," she gasped. "Get if off, or we'll both go under."

He fumbled at the catches, his fingers dulled by cold. The water pulled at him like a sea monster's claw, and he heard Chitto groaning behind him. Finally the breastplate came off, but Chitto lost her grip on whatever she had a hold of, and they were borne off by the flood, branches and deadfall tearing at their exposed flesh.

After what seemed like forever, the current lessened, and they fetched against something. Together they crawled up onto a bank that rose a few feet from the flood. The rain lessened, and thunder growled on, but only in the distance. The water rose another six centimeters and then began to subside.

"Thanks," he managed.

"It's all good," Chitto said.

"Except the bit where we just lost everything," he said. "Weapons, supplies, the truck."

"Nitpicker," Chitto replied.

But he was right. When it was clear enough to look around, the truck was nowhere to be seen—nor was there any sign of the rest of the squad.

* * *

Before nightfall they found a road running generally south, although they couldn't be certain it was the same highway they had been on earlier. Amar was relieved to discover that both of them still had their sidearms, and so they weren't completely helpless. But he felt like a walking bruise, and his every joint and juncture felt aflame, chapped by his wet, stiff clothes.

Making camp involved little more than finding the highest, driest place they could to take turns sleeping. They still had their radio transceivers, but they were short range, and there was nothing but static on the frequencies they used.

The night was wet, hot, and miserable, and he didn't get much in the way of sleep, but in the gray hours before morning, his radio finally started talking to him—not with a human voice, but with the dots and dashes of Morse code. The signal repeated six times, then gave way to static.

"Did you get that?" Chitto asked. "I haven't had time to learn the code."

"Yeah," he said. "We've got a rally point."

* * *

In the truck, the longleaf pine and oak that was reclaiming the land blurred into a continuous screen, obscuring the contents of the young forest. On foot, you saw more. The rusting cars, the crumbling churches, the faded billboards, water towers proclaiming the names of towns few remembered ever existing.

Oakdale was one such town. The sign cheerfully declaring they were entering it was still there, peeking through the understory.

"Rally point is about a kilometer ahead," Amar told Chitto. "Near the old town center."

They had covered about half that distance when his radio started prattling again, this time urging him to approach with caution. It came a bit belated, because by that time he could hear the screams.

Oakdale wasn't like Greenville and Helena, settlements that ADVENT grudgingly tolerated. Oakdale was far too deep in a contagion zone. It should have been empty, and from the looks of it, it had been until recently. It was poor even by shantytown standards, consisting of a handful of tents, some tarps thrown over the holes in the roofs of existing buildings, and a few small solar arrays. Also glaringly present were two ADVENT aerial transports. The troopers were rounding the settlers up and marching them—or, in some cases, carrying—them into the transports.

And not all the captives were settlers: Toby, DeLao, and Lena were among them.

"Shit!" Chitto yelped, and then her pistol went off. He spun around and saw she was shooting at a jabber only a few meters away. It had a stun lance in its hand. Chitto fired again but came nowhere near hitting the thing. From the corner of his eye, he saw another one charging up on his right like a berserker.

He jerked his pistol up and fired twice. The first bullet hit the jabber in the neck and the second right in the face. He was turning to fire at the second when he felt a searing pain in the back of his shoulder. His whole body spasmed, and he dropped his pistol as he fell to the ground. It felt like his blood had been pumped out and replaced with lava. Groaning, he rolled, reaching for the fallen weapon, but he knew there was no time. He heard Chitto firing wildly. The trooper raised her lance.

Then her head came off. Dazed by the pain, he watched curiously as it bounced on the ground, and the body that had once worn it dropped to its knees.

Nishimura grinned down at him, her small mouth bent in a devilish grin, her eyes bright beneath her sable brows, and then she was off again, bloody sword gripped in one hand.

He picked up his weapon, trying to ignore the agony

that had been burned into his flesh, but it took a few moments to regain his motor skills. He knew he was lucky that he hadn't passed out, but somehow it didn't feel that way.

When he did manage to get up, he saw that more fighting was going on near the transports, but he couldn't make out the details. Nishimura was no longer in sight, but she'd left another corpse behind her—the jabber who had stabbed him.

He glanced at Chitto, who looked a little shaken. "You got it together?" he asked.

"Yeah," she said. "Sorry."

"Don't be sorry," he told her. "Just keep your head. See that brick building up there? Move up. I'll cover you."

She was about halfway there when a mag blast speared toward her, narrowly missing her shoulder and cutting a sapling in half. He saw the jabber and began firing at it. It was about twenty meters away, so his first shot missed. His second bullet connected before the trooper crouched down behind a tree. Chitto made it to the building and fired at it from two meters away. He saw chips fly from a nearby oak.

No wonder she had been issued a shotgun. Chitto had terrible aim.

The jabber stood up again, and he shot it twice more. It staggered back, and then Amar heard a burst from an assault rifle. The trooper shuddered and went down.

Amar saw Dux about ten meters off to his right, giving him a thumb's up.

In a few more minutes it was over. There had only been

eight jabbers to begin with, and most had been armed with stun lances. They hadn't expected heavy resistance, and probably no resistance at all, not from a group this small and impoverished.

He gradually sorted out what had happened as DeLao looked over his wound and the rest tried to sort some semblance of order into the panicked settlers.

Toby, DeLao, and Lena had reached the rendezvous first and found it occupied. They didn't know they had walked inside the ADVENT perimeter and had been surprised pretty much the way he and Chitto had, only there had been no Nishimura to pull their asses out of the fire. Thomas, Dux, and Nishimura arrived next, and had been working out a strategy when he and Chitto showed up.

"Took a ding out of your scapula," DeLao told him. "Nothing that'll kill you right away."

Dux was in worse shape. At some point in the final moments of the battle, he had taken a glancing hit on his gut. He still had his armor, and it had saved his life, but bits of it had vaporized and blown through one of his lungs. He was bearing up for the moment, but it was the sort of wound that would definitely not get better on its own or with the resources they had. They now had another reason to find Sam's XCOM facility.

"Mister."

He glanced up to find a boy of perhaps seven years looking at him. He was thin and had a couple of gaps in his teeth.

"Yes?"

"Thank you for what you done."

"It's okay," he said.

The boy continued to stand there.

"Are y'all going to stay with us?" he asked.

Amar looked around. "No," he said. "We can't. We have something we have to do a long way from here."

"Well, can I come with you then?"

"I bet your mom and dad wouldn't want that," Amar said.

"They ain't got no say in the matter," the boy replied. "They got took last year."

Amar swore silently and then swayed to his feet. "Do you guys have a leader?" he asked.

"I reckon that would be Mr. Deloach over there," the boy told him.

Deloach was thirty-something. He had a mane of dirty blond hair and arms that looked as if they had been made of wire and rubber.

"You're Deloach?" Amar asked.

"Yes, sir," Deloach said. "We're awful grateful for what you've done here."

"That's great," he said. "But you need to get these people—these kids—to one of the settlements. It's not safe out here."

"Don't much care for the settlements," the man said. "Can't hear myself think."

"A boy just told me his parents were taken last year," Amar persisted. "Where was that?"

"Down in Atchafalaya Basin," he said.

"Another contagion zone."

"I ain't lettin' no damn aliens tell me where I can and

cannot live," Deloach snapped.

"I understand that," Amar said, starting to heat up. "I just killed two of their troopers. You think I'm on their side? But understand, when they find you out here, they do not take you to a settlement. They do not take you to a city. They take you, and no one ever sees you again. Ever."

"I got news for you," Deloach said. "The settlements ain't safe, either."

"It's better than being out here," Amar said. He turned away, disgusted, and nearly ran into Lena, who was standing there with tears running down her face.

"It's real, isn't it?" she said. "Everything you've been saying."

"You think?" he said, and brushed by her.

* * *

None of the vehicles operated after the flood. The other pickup had a broken axle, and the van was likewise totaled. The others had managed to salvage some of the supplies and weapons, but once again they were on foot. Fortunately, according to Sam, they could probably walk it in two days. He was right, but they were two very long, hot days of biting flies, mosquitoes, and leeches. They saw a cottonmouth big enough to eat a cat. A big cat. Everyone else seemed pretty impressed, but Amar had grown up with cobras.

ADVENT patrols grew more frequent as they approached the Gulf of Mexico, so they stayed adjacent to the road rather than on it when they could.

Dux couldn't walk by the end of the first day, so they built a litter and took turns carrying him. Amar noticed that Lena took a turn like everyone else.

When she was done, he walked up beside her.

"Hey," he said.

"KB," she said. She hesitated and then plunged on.

"I'm sorry about the other night," she said. "I wouldn't have . . . I pulled the trigger by accident when you hit me."

"That's fine," he said. "I never met a pretty girl who didn't try to kill me at some point."

She fingered her mud-streaked hair and glanced at her filthy clothes.

"That was supposed to be a joke," he said.

"The part about me being pretty, or about girls trying to kill you?" she asked.

"Never mind," he said. "It's just something I used to say."

"Anyway," she said. "I'm sorry." She looked up at him, and her green eyes caught him. He held her gaze for what felt like too long.

He finally looked down, feeling embarrassed.

"In your position, I probably would have done the same thing," he said.

"You came up to me, just now," she said. "Did you have something to say?"

"Yeah," he said. "I wanted to tell you that for someone who grew up in a city, you're hanging in there pretty well. You're kind of tough."

"If you could be inside of my skin for a while, you wouldn't think so," she said. "But thanks."

* * *

On the evening of the second day, they reached the settlement of Sunflower. Toby and Nishimura went in to see if it was safe, and they were all in by dusk. What passed for a doctor there said he couldn't do much more for Dux than make him more comfortable.

And there was Lena. Amar found her sitting near a patch of bare dirt, where some girls were skipping rope. He mentally braced himself and then sat down beside her. She had washed up and traded her clothes for a pair of brown pants and a stained blue shirt.

"Why did you stow away back in Helena?" he asked her. "Why didn't you just stay there or go back to Gulf City?"

She didn't look at him, and for a while she didn't say anything.

"I had to know what my sister died for," she said. "I wanted to understand. I still do."

He nodded. "Okay," he said. "Do you?"

"I don't know."

"Then you don't," he said, as gently as he could. "And you can't come any farther with us."

"Why not?"

"Right now, if ADVENT picks you up, you can't tell them anything all that important," he said. "In another day, that will change."

"And you'll have to what—make sure I can't talk?"

He sighed. "Something like that."

"I see." She sounded cold. He didn't blame her.

"Just make it easy on yourself," he said. "Stay here. They'll take care of you until you figure it all out."

* * *

But the next morning, she was there, stubbornly lifting one end of Dux's litter.

Sam frowned and glanced at Thomas, who shrugged. Amar expected an argument about it, but instead they started on.

About a kilometer down the road, however, things came to a head, when Sam drew his sidearm and pointed it at Lena.

"Okay," he said. "Turn around and walk back the settlement. You'll be fine. They'll take care of you."

Lena looked pale. Amar could see her lip quivering. But she didn't move.

"Why here?" she asked. "Why did you let me leave the settlement with you? Is it because you wanted to be out of earshot of Sunflower when you shot me?"

"Nobody has to get shot," Sam replied. "But you aren't going another step with us."

"But if I do?"

"I'll do what I have to," he replied.

Lena was about a meter to his right. Amar stepped to place himself between her and Sam.

"What the hell is this, KB?" Sam demanded.

"I'm not going to watch you kill an unarmed human," he said. "And if you are who you say you are—and belong to the organization you say you do—you won't do it."

"You don't understand," he said. "If you knew what I was protecting—"

"It wouldn't change anything," Amar interrupted. "I still wouldn't let you shoot her."

"Put your gun away, Sam," Thomas said. "That's an order."

"I don't answer to you," Sam replied.

"Today you do," she said.

Amar kept his gaze locked on Sam's. He felt strange, almost serene, and each breath seemed to go on for a century.

Sam lowered the gun and looked past him at Lena.

"I can't promise anything once we get there, Lena," he said. "The decision won't be in my hands anymore." He nodded his head toward Thomas. "Or theirs."

"I understand," she said.

"I really hope you do."

* * *

Half an hour later they reached the densely vegetated banks of the Sabine River. Across the water the remains of an old oil refinery slept beneath a blanket of rust. The aliens had power sources that had rendered fossil fuels relatively useless for that purpose, although some petroleum was still used in manufacturing plastics and such.

Was this really where the XCOM base was? Hidden in this ruin? So close to the coastal cities? He could see three aircraft at the moment, although none were directly overhead. How could they possibly have avoided detection for twenty years?

Sam was talking to someone on his radio. It seemed that this was the place.

"Well?" Thomas said.

"In a moment," Sam replied.

It was a long moment. Amar watched across the river, looking for a door to open, someone walking toward them. . . .

A cormorant sitting on a stick in the water suddenly took wing. Amar was wondering what had startled the bird when he realized the stick was growing taller, and then he understood that it wasn't a stick, but a pipe of some sort.

Then something large emerged, gunmetal gray, flange-shaped, and now the water was mounding, as if a whale was surfacing.

Or a submarine.

"*Asu!*" Nishimura gasped.

"What she said," DeLao said.

"Ladies and gentlemen," Sam said, "I give you the Elpis."

Part II
The Elpis

"The mouse-deer may forget the trap, but the trap will not forget the mouse-deer."

—MALAY PROVERB

CHAPTER 7

THE ELPIS HAD old bones. The bulk of her dated to the first decade after World War II, nearly a hundred years ago, when diesel submarines were state of the art. But the atomic age was unfolding and as nuclear subs became the front line in underwater technology, the older vessels were gradually refitted or retired to shipyards, museums, and scrapheaps.

"It would have been easier to obtain a nuclear sub, actually," Sam told them. He was obviously excited about and proud of the ship.

At the moment they were in a conference room, waiting to be debriefed, and Sam—always talkative—was now practically blabbering. It was possible he was in part trying to repair his mistake in threatening Lena. No one in the squad really trusted her, but Natives did not kill humans, and threatening to do so had lost him any goodwill he might have gained since conscripting them.

So now he was trying to impress them with the amazing place where they now found themselves, to show them that his attempts to protect it were justified or at least understandable.

Amar was impressed, but he wasn't yet convinced.

However, Sam was still working on it.

"The thing about a nuclear sub," he was saying, "is it emits neutrinos, and the aliens are very good at tracking neutrino sources. It doesn't occur to them that anything dangerous to them could run on technology this old. But there's more here than meets the eye. . . ."

He didn't finish the lecture, because the door opened, and Sam bounded to his feet. Thomas was close behind him.

The man in the doorway was on the frail side, nearly bald, with mere wisps of gray hair along the fringes of his skull. But behind his wire-rimmed glasses his eyes were lively and intelligent.

As he stepped into the room, he was followed by a much younger fellow with a shock of red hair and an expression that was probably meant to be neutral but which to Amar seemed somehow disapproving.

"Dr. Shen!" Thomas said. It was the most excited he thought he had ever seen her.

"You look familiar," the old man said, studying her intently. His lips curled in a little smile. "Thomas, yes? Holly Thomas?"

"I'm flattered you remember me, sir," she said.

"You were one of the Commander's favorites," he said. "Because you were one of our best. I'm so glad you're still with us. Gladder still that you have joined us here on the Elpis."

"I think it was only because I mentioned your name that Captain Thomas agreed to escort me here," Sam said.

Shen's features fell a bit as he surveyed the rest of the squad. "Sam, is it true that you are the only survivor of your expedition?"

"Yes, sir," he said. "We were ambushed by ADVENT troopers. Captain Thomas and her squad saved my life and escorted me back to the Elpis."

"How convenient that they were nearby," the red-headed man said.

A look of irritation flashed across Thomas's face, but she quickly mastered it.

"When Sam told me that you were still alive, sir, it seemed too good to be true." She paused, looked at the floor, then raised her gaze again. "Sir, is the Commander . . ."

Shen shook his head. "There has never been any word of him, and I have searched, believe me. But there is also no conclusive proof that he is dead—so there is always hope, you know. Elpis."

"Sir?"

Dr. Shen smiled.

"Do you remember the ancient Greek story of Pandora's box? How she was given a chest but forbidden to open it? But of course she couldn't resist, and when she finally broke the seals, all of the sorrows, disasters, diseases, and misfortunes that plague us now escaped. When she finally managed to close it, only one thing remained in the box: Elpis. Hope." He waved his arms around the ship. "This is our Elpis. The Commander may be missing, but others have survived. I've spent many years trying to find them, to recover data, to gather new information. To rebuild XCOM. And I believe we are very near succeeding."

He took a seat, and the red-headed man sat beside him.

"So, as the rest of you have no doubt gathered, my name is Shen, Raymond Shen. I had the honor of being chief engineer back in the old days. This is our ship's captain, Ahti Laaksonen."

"Good day, all," Laaksonen said.

Sam made a round of introductions, and then Shen got down to business.

"Sam, what do you have to report?"

"Hold up," Laaksonen interposed. "Sam, what have you told them already?"

"Only that I was looking for something in the old facility. But not what."

"Then perhaps the three of us—Dr. Shen, you, myself—ought to review your findings before making them available to men and women we know very little about." He nodded to Thomas. "No disrespect intended. But we must be very careful."

Thomas's expression was unreadable.

"As Dr. Shen wishes," she said.

The old man looked them over. "Captain Thomas, it's been a long time, but I have no doubts about you. Do you vouch for your people?"

Thomas nodded toward Lena. "Ms. Bishop is a civilian, sir. We found her in ADVENT custody and brought her along for her own protection. If you're going to tell us anything classified, I suggest she be removed from the conversation."

"Classified?" Laaksonen repeated in an icy tone. "The

existence of this ship is classified. The survival of Dr. Shen is classified as well. She is now privy to any number of classified things. Is she from one of the cities? Did you at least have the sense to remove her chip?"

"It had already been removed," Thomas said, "by locals in the Greenville settlement."

"Dr. Shen—" Laaksonen began, but the older man cut him off.

"Young lady," Shen told Lena, "I'm going to have you escorted to the Rathskeller or, if you prefer, the showers, if you would like to tidy up. The rest of you will remain. Captain Dixon and his squad would have been privy to this conversation, and I think you should know what they died for and what you fought for."

A young woman with a sidearm stepped in from the hall and motioned for Lena to follow her.

"Thank you, Doctor," Lena said. "A shower would be nice."

When she was gone, Shen knitted his fingers and placed his elbows on the table.

"Sam?" he said.

Sam was trying to keep his expression neutral, but he couldn't keep from smiling.

"I found it, sir," he said.

Shen closed his eyes and expressed a deep sigh. "I had hoped," he said. "Sam, this is good news."

"Yes, sir."

"I feel I must still raise an objection—" Laaksonen began, but Shen shook his head.

"In the first few weeks of the war," he said, "we made

some gains. It was clear that the alien technology was vastly superior to ours, and that to beat them we would have to understand it, come up to speed, and build our own version of it. We gathered scraps left from skirmishes fought with aliens as they abducted people. But we also managed to shoot down two of their aircraft. The first we found to be in excellent condition, but we were unable to maintain a position at its crash site long enough to study it. The second — and last — crashed during the final hours of the war, as our own systems were being compromised. The satellite data of its trajectory was destroyed at our command facility. I thought the information might have been backed up somewhere else. As it turns out, I was right. True, Sam?"

"Yes," Sam said. "I have the location. It's in a very remote spot, far from any of the New Cities. Chances are good that it's still there."

Shen swept his gaze around the table. "You understand what this would mean, I hope. I have managed to survive for this long because my base is mobile. But it isn't sufficient. If I had access to an alien ship, if we could get it flying again . . ."

"That's a lot of ifs," Thomas remarked.

"Indeed," the doctor replied. "Even if we can't repair it, we would still have access to their technology in a setting that will allow us the time to study and hopefully reproduce it. I once had my qualms about this; frankly, in some respects I still do. I was once afraid that if we used their means we would become too much like them. I still feel that way about their biotech, to some extent. But the past twenty years have convinced me that we cannot defeat them with minor raids here and there or by hacking their propaganda. It may further our cause, yes. But sooner or later, we must fight—go to war—to regain our world. This we simply cannot do with the weapons and materials available to us. Finding that ship is a huge step in achieving the capabilities we require."

"So that's where we're headed next?" Thomas asked. "The downed ship?"

"Not quite," Shen said, with a sparkle in his eye. "There is a stop we must make along the way."

* * *

Amar hit the showers after the meeting, his head more than slightly awhirl, but the hot water—*hot water!*—settled him back down. The blue shirt and ivory pants provided to him were soft and clean, and although part of him was dog-tired, he was also hungry enough to eat a live cobra head-first.

He hadn't any idea how the submarine had been laid out originally, but he was willing to bet this one had been significantly remodeled. The lighting was modern, and while there were no windows or portholes or whatever ships had, there were LED panels at intervals that were obviously tied to cameras outside. He stopped for a moment to wonder at the pale blue water through which they were moving, at the silvery clouds of fish fleeing their approach.

He reflected that the Elpis was indeed amazing, on

its own terms, but it was like a stone knife in a world dominated by nuclear weapons.

But even a stone knife was deadly in the right hands.

The Rathskeller was on the upper of two decks and was very much like a pub. It was small—the ship was around ninety-five meters long, but it was only eight wide—and currently nearly fully occupied, largely by his squad. His choices of drink were beer, water, juice, hot tea, or coffee. He chose the beer and was happy to discover that, while it was bit skunky, it was actually beer, and it was cold. Dinner was a choice of salt cod, tofu, or lentils, pasta or rice, green beans or cabbage, all served from a buffet station by a bespectacled little bearded man who spoke very little English and none of Amar's other tongues.

The tofu looked best, and it was surprisingly good, covered in a red chili, lime, and fish sauce. He sat across from Lena, who was alone at a small table, picking at the lentils. She looked clean; her hair was combed and she had changed from the settlement clothing in which he'd last seen her into a green T-shirt and gray pants.

"Better than squirrel?" he asked.

She shrugged.

"The tofu is good," he said. "It's made from beans, not animals."

"I'll remember that," she said. Then she put down her fork and looked at him directly. He noticed her green eyes had flecks of gold in them.

"Thank you," she said. "I can honestly say no one has ever stood between me and a gun before. I was really quite . . . overwhelmed."

"Sam was never going to shoot you," he said. "I just had to make him understand that."

He was uncomfortable with her earnest gaze and turned his own to his food.

"You're a good man," she said.

It felt surprisingly good to hear her say that—perhaps in part because it was so unexpected—but probably more because he hadn't realized that he *cared* what her opinion of him was.

Yet he did, and he felt like he should respond to her.

"My father once told me he had only one goal in raising me," he said. "It wasn't for me to be rich or powerful or even brave, but to be good."

"He must be proud, then," she said.

"I think he would be disappointed," Amar said. "I don't know—can't know—because he went out one day to hunt, and he never came back. I was ten, and I swore then I would join the resistance as soon as they would take me."

Her expression shifted, became more melancholy and something else he couldn't pin down.

"I'm sorry to hear about your father," she said. "But your reaction, I can understand that."

"But the thing is I didn't join the Natives to fight for an ideal or to help people. I joined because I wanted to avenge him by killing aliens—to kill in the name of my father, the man who never hurt anyone and never would, except to protect his family. He lived a life of grace and peace, and I know in my heart he died that way."

He realized he had never said any of this out loud to anyone before. He wasn't sure why he was doing it now.

Maybe it was because she was a non-com. If he brought this up with Nishimura or Dux, they would probably think he was whinging. Everyone who did what they did had issues, but you were expected not to bother other people with yours.

Now she looked puzzled.

"Then . . . you don't believe in this cause that you fight for?" she asked.

"That was then," he said. "Before I met these guys. Thomas, Rider . . ." he trailed off. "Now I've seen some of what ADVENT does with my own eyes. I know we're doing what we have to. But I've seen people die. And I've killed. The ADVENT soldiers—they aren't human. But they look like they might be part human, some kind of bioengineered hybrid. I don't know what's in those suits, if they're human or robots or something else. Do they feel anything? Do they miss their comrades when I kill them? I don't know these things."

She took a drink of her beer. "This is confusing for me. You know that."

"I understand," he said.

"I'm not sure you do," she said. "I had cancer. I was eighteen years old, and my life was over. Gene therapy saved me. How am I not supposed to be grateful for that? And all of the things you're saying—your father wanting you to be good, you with your moral dilemma—that's not how we . . . how people in the New Cities think of you. You're the barbarians pounding at the gate, hackers trying to ruin the good life. When people go missing, you're the ones they blame. And up until now, I didn't have any doubts about any of that. But if it's all a lie . . . Where are they all going? Upward of a thousand people went missing in Gulf City last year. If you guys aren't doing it, then who is?"

"I think the answer is obvious," he said. "I've seen some of the ADVENT facilities, spied on them, set up monitoring equipment to count the faces of those who arrive and those who leave. Only none of them ever leave. And we don't know what they do there. At least, I don't. Maybe Dr. Shen does."

She took a few more bites, looking thoughtful.

"Thomas told Shen ADVENT was holding me," she said. "You told me I was captured by smugglers."

"That's right," he said. "The guys in the bar probably drugged you. Then they took you up to their hideaway to remove your chip. That's what we think, anyway. But then an ADVENT patrol came across them. The black market guys were all dead when we got there. You were alive."

"So the troopers found me there," she mused. "Do you think they would have taken me off to one of those facilities you're talking about? To do whatever they do?"

"What do you think?" he asked.

She sighed and put her hand to her brow. "Why didn't you tell me about this before?"

He shrugged. "At first I didn't want to frighten you. After that, well, you wouldn't have believed us, would you?"

"I guess not," she admitted.

"So what now? First all you wanted to do was get away from us. Then you were willing to risk death to tag along. What's your next act?"

She was silent for a moment.

"There is something I didn't tell you," she said. "My

sister wasn't the first person I lost. My mother disappeared three years ago. She went to the Atlantic Seaboard, and I never saw her again. She was supposed to have been killed during a dissident attack. But in her case, I never saw the body." She looked at him frankly. "Maybe she's still out there. Maybe if I'm with you guys I can at least find out the truth."

"Maybe," he said. "Like Shen said, we can always hope. And if you're joining us, that's a better reason than revenge. But it's still not enough."

"It will have to do for now," she said.

CHAPTER 8

THE ELPIS HAD a crew of seventy-two, including Amar's squad, which made the ship feel rather small at times. Amar had never been much for small spaces, so he tried to quell his claustrophobia and fill his time learning more about XCOM, its history, the plans they were making.

Each Native cell had its own quirks, and these people were no different, except they had a deeper connection to the real thing. Sure, Thomas had been with XCOM, but her experience was almost exclusively military.

Their cell had coordinated with others in times past. They had sabotaged railways, looted food stockpiles, rescued more groups like the people in Oakdale than he cared to think about, because that only reminded him of the ones they didn't manage to protect — the empty camps, the occasional mass graves they came across.

But there had only been the vaguest idea of a bigger plan. It was hard to organize.

They had their Morse code network and various ways of hiding information inside of what was ostensibly entertainment radio. Some cells had managed to hack into jabber propaganda and contradict it, but he wasn't sure how much good that did. Lena wasn't stupid, but she'd still been convinced the aliens were well intentioned, despite the occasional dissident broadcast claiming the contrary.

XCOM had been far more than a military organization. They had built infrastructure, done research and development, sought sources of funding and managed those funds to best advantage.

And in the end, they had failed. The governments that underwrote them lost faith in their ability to hold the aliens at bay—much less beat them—and folded. And that was very much how things still stood, with each region ruled by puppet regimes of collaborators.

But it didn't take a genius to understand that Shen had found funding somewhere, and that didn't just show in the ship itself. The Elpis carried a research lab in her bow.

Which is where he met the *other* Dr. Shen.

He guessed she was in early thirties. She had her father's onyx hair and a quiet intensity. She was never still, always tinkering with a widget, running computations, tuning the ship's engines. Not the sort of person who would drop everything to give you a tour. But she didn't mind talking as she went about her seemingly endless tasks. And she spoke Mandarin as well as English, which was nice to hear after all this time.

But most of the time it almost seemed like she was talking to herself, even when answering a question. As if he wasn't really quite there. She almost never stopped what she was doing to make eye contact.

He asked her about the ship's weapons once, and she made a dismissive little clicking sound.

"Yes, we have the deck guns," she said, "and we did retain minor torpedo capability, although what we bear is much smaller and deadlier than this ship originally carried. I'm standing where the forward torpedo batteries were. The fact is, the ship isn't at all about fighting. It's about hiding. If they ever really know where we are, they won't come within torpedo or gun range. They will torch us from the sky.

"So what have we been working on? Buffers to reduce engine sound. Filters to minimize the exhaust from burning diesel. The hull is wired with a stealth system that passes sixty percent of low-level energy emissions — like radar — around us rather than bouncing them back. We're not transparent, but we are translucent.

"But the number one thing that keeps us safe is that the enemy doesn't know we exist. So, weapons? We are already carrying more than we need."

The rest of the crew were standoffish at first, especially the soldiers, who consciously or unconsciously resented them for taking the places of their friends and comrades, and especially resented that Thomas was now the ranking officer.

But the fact was that despite having better armor and better weapons, what remained of Elpis's soldiers were on the green side, some having never seen any combat at all. Thomas dealt with that — and with the general boredom and restlessness that seemed inevitable on a voyage like this—by holding training sessions in close combat. When they surfaced, they went topside and took target practice and worked on basic tactics and communication.

Thomas had a style of command that got its results not from fear and intimidation, but rather from making you not want to let her down, and she was good at seeing the personalities of a squad and putting the right people together.

Usually. She had been right about Rider. Chitto, Amar still wasn't sure about. She had guts, and she had saved his life probably, back in the flood—but she couldn't hit the sub if she put the muzzle of her weapon against it, and she too often tended to act on her own, without consulting with anyone, including her partner.

Like the time she'd let Lena get the shotgun.

After the first week, Lena asked if she could participate in the drills, and Thomas put her in.

One day, after training, Thomas called Amar up to where she stood on the bow. Her fading blonde hair was in its usual long braid, but the strip above her forehead that she usually kept shaved was growing back in a bit.

"What's up, Chief?" he asked.

"Just checking in," she said.

"What do you mean?" he asked.

She fidgeted with her half-ear. "You know me," she said. "I'm not much on sharing and all that. But I know you took losing Rider hard."

"I'm fine, Chief," he said. "I'm doing my job okay, right?"

"Sure," she said. "Better than okay. But you used be . . .

well, funny. Made jokes, told stories, poked fun at people. Now I rarely see you smile."

"You don't do any of that stuff, Chief," he said. "At least not much."

"True," she said. "But I never did. It's not in my nature." She sighed and looked out to sea. "We all have switches in us," she said. "To do what we do, sometimes we have to turn those switches off. But we also have to learn to turn them back on. You're not just a soldier to me, KB. You're *my* soldier."

"I appreciate that, Chief," he said.

He remembered his talk with Lena, his assumption that any complaint he made to his squad mates would be seen as a sign of weakness. Maybe he had undersold them— after all, they were the closest thing he had to a family.

"What I'm saying," Thomas went on, "is if you need to talk to someone, do it. I don't mean me. I'm terrible at this stuff."

"Okay, Chief," he said. "Is that all?"

"Not quite," she said. "I'd like you to start leading some exercises."

That came from a blind direction.

"Why me?" he asked.

"Because I see potential in you," she replied. "I think one day you'll make a fine squad leader. Why do you think I stuck you with Chitto? With any of the others, you would just follow their leads. With her, you have to learn to command."

So that was why. He knew there had to be something. But command?

"Begging your pardon, Chief," he said, "I don't think I'm the leader type."

"Exactly," she said. "If you thought so, you wouldn't be."

She clapped him on the shoulder and walked back toward the hatch, leaving him to wonder whether she was serious, kidding, or had just passed along a koan for him to contemplate.

* * *

The Elpis plowed along, on the sea and under it. They made much faster time on top of the water, averaging about eighteen or twenty kilometers an hour. Underwater, it was more like four.

As the trip wore on and they left inhabited lands farther behind, they spent more time on the surface, especially after dark.

One such night Amar lay on his back and watched the slow wheel of the stars, wondering at their beauty. The sea was calm, and the air was decidedly chilly.

He was remembering that some people believed the souls of the dead became stars. It seemed like a nice thought. If it were so, which would Rider be? The faint red one there, or the brash, actinic one near the horizon?

"May I join you?"

He saw Lena's silhouette against the night sky.

"Sure," he said.

She sat cross-legged beside him. "I never really saw the stars in Gulf City," she said, looking up. "There's always light. But this . . . this is gorgeous."

"You should see them from the high desert or the mountains," he said. "With air so thin and dry—it's almost like being in space."

"I would like to see that," she said. "Although it's hard to imagine them being brighter than this. Do you know the constellations?"

"Yes, some of them. I grew up just north of the equator. From there you can see all of the constellations in the Northern Hemisphere and most of the southern ones. We're starting to lose the northern stars."

"Do you mean we're in the Southern Hemisphere?" she asked.

"Yeah," he said. "We've been going south since we got clear of the gulf, and now it's starting to get cold."

"Where do you think we're going? Antarctica?"

"I don't know the specific destination any more than you do," he said. "But we're pretty far south, from what I can tell."

She looked back up at the stars. "I wonder which one they came from," she said. "The aliens."

Oddly, he hadn't thought about that since he was a kid. She was right; they had come from somewhere, and there was a chance at any given moment that he was looking at the homeland of their oppressors.

"Lena," he sighed, "you really know how to kill a mood."

She laughed, and he realized that it was the first time he'd heard her do so. He liked the sound of it. He remembered his conversation with Thomas, about how he never joked anymore.

Maybe his switch was resetting.

"Sorry," she said. "Not the first time I've been accused of that."

"It's okay," he said. "Before you showed up, my mood was about to take a bad turn anyway. I was thinking about a friend of mine."

"The woman who was killed rescuing Sam?"

"That's a good guess," he said. "Who told you about that?"

"DeLao. He said you were taking it pretty hard."

"I think I'm taking it just fine," he said.

First Thomas, now DeLao. Were they all talking about this?

"We were close," he admitted.

"Were you lovers?"

For a moment he was flat-out stunned.

"What kind of question is that?" he asked. "Why would you ask me that?"

"Auugggh," she said. "There I go again. I thought . . . I guess I thought you might want to talk about it." She paused. "And I guess I'm curious. About you."

What did that mean? he wondered. Her face was faint in the starlight, difficult to read. But she felt closer somehow. She was still sitting on the deck, and he was still lying down. Was she leaning over him?

"Curious about what?" he asked.

"Like, what's your real name? It can't be KB. That's just your pirate name."

"Amar," he said. "My mother named me Amar."

"I like it," she said. "What does it mean?"

He felt a faint smile on his face. "It can mean either tranquility or strife," he said.

"Kind of a conflicted name," she said.

"I suppose," he said. "What does 'Lena' mean?"

"I have no idea," she replied. "I'm named after my great-grandmother. But I like your name. It suits you."

She laid down beside him, and her hand fell so it was just touching his. Something akin to an electric jolt shocked through his entire body. For a moment he felt like he couldn't breathe.

She didn't move her hand, and after a moment her fingers moved to twine with his, and without really thinking, he gripped back.

They stayed like that, silently, for a long moment. Then she rolled onto her side so that she was facing him. Her face was very close, and he could feel the warmth of her breath.

"No," he said. "Rider and I weren't lovers. Maybe in another world, if we had met on a dance floor instead of downrange. But being that kind of involved with someone in your squad . . . it isn't a good idea. It can make you sloppy."

For a moment he saw her eyes clearly, bright stars shining in a nebula. Then she laid back down and returned her gaze to the stars.

"I see," she said. "Yes, I can see how it might."

She sounded disappointed, and he knew he was, and in that moment he wanted to go back to before he'd said anything.

Instead he just uncurled his fingers from hers.

* * *

Three days later, Thomas called them together.

"Tomorrow morning," she informed them. "O-four hundred, full gear. We're going ashore."

He noticed she had shaved her bangs again.

* * *

"I feel so pretty," DeLao said, examining himself in his new armor. Mostly new, anyway. They had all been measured for new stuff, but if they had, say, a chest plate still in decent shape, Shen just worked it in.

Their supplies weren't unlimited, but even more to the point, the three weeks they had spent at sea—as long as it had seemed—still wasn't that much time in which to fabricate full suits of armor, not with the scale of the engineering equipment and personnel present on the Elpis. Still, Amar had to agree they were at least 60 percent spiffier than before.

And a little safer.

* * *

The Elpis surfaced under an overcast sky. It was bitterly cold, and Amar was happy Shen had given them insulated body suits to go beneath their armor.

The ship lay off the lee side of an island that was the single most uninviting place he had ever seen. A truncated volcanic cone formed its core, and most of it was covered in snow and ice. What wasn't frozen over looked mostly like black gravel. The overall impression was that of a really filthy snowball, dropped from a height into a cold blue sea. From what he could see, the island was tiny, no more than a few kilometers in diameter.

A few elephant seals reclined on the stony beach, and maybe half a million birds, most of which were penguins of some kind. The smell of them was unbelievable, enough to bring tears to his eyes.

"What's she doing?" DeLao wondered. Amar saw Lena emerging from the hatch, just behind Sam. She had on a parka and flak jacket, but she didn't appear to be armed.

"Dr. Shen—the older one—asked if we could take her along," Thomas said. "So I don't want to hear anything else about it."

"Fine," DeLao grumbled. Their body suits had parka-style hoods. DeLao had his on but was wearing his Red Devils cap over it.

"Antarctica?" Toby wondered aloud, taking in the island through the scope on his rifle.

"Or pretty close," Amar said.

"There's nothing here," Toby muttered.

"That's the point," Sam said. He glanced around at the party, which included the usual squad minus Dux, who was a great deal better but not yet ready for combat. Carrying the rocket launcher in his place was a massive man named Aleki Palepoi. His face was soft, kind-looking, and didn't really seem to fit his size. One of his arms and half of his chest were covered in complex blackwork tattoos.

"We shouldn't see any action here," Sam told them.

"But better safe than sorry."

"I don't know," Nishimura said. "Those penguins look pretty suspicious. If they start glowing, shoot to kill."

"And the smell," Amar said. "That can't be of this world."

"It's called *guano*," DeLao said. "You'd best get used to it."

"All the time I've spent with you," Amar said, "you'd think I *would* be used to it."

The nose of the Elpis was edged over a metal platform built up from the shore. They climbed down and in a few moments were standing on the desolate shingle.

Sam seemed to be looking for something, and Thomas didn't say anything about going anywhere, so they milled around a little. The birds and seals watched them, and some of the former even waddled over, near enough for him to kick one if he wanted to, but the birds didn't seem at all concerned that he would.

"Heads up," Nishimura said.

Across the beach, three vehicles were moving toward them, parting the sea of penguins. As they drew nearer, Amar saw two of them were jeeps and the third a large flatbed truck. The latter pulled up as near the sub as possible, and the crew of the Elpis began lowering crates onto the bed with one of the two cranes the ship sported.

The jeeps were for them. Once the truck was loaded, they piled in and started out along the beach.

The drivers seemed human enough and eager to talk. Amar's was named Eduardo and had a lot of questions about what was going on elsewhere in the world. The island was too far away from any place, he said, to receive the usual radio programs.

Amar filled him in when he could, but Eduardo mostly wanted to know about Argentina, and Amar had never been there. He remembered a few things from the radio—there had been a riot in one of the settlements, and they were doing okay in the underground football league.

Amar revised his estimate of the island to about five kilometers at its widest, and was just starting to wonder if they were going to circumnavigate it when the vehicles took a right turn toward the volcano.

At first, he could not imagine what their destination was: The mountain was far too steep to drive up.

But as they came nearer he saw that what he had initially taken to be part of the icy mountainside was actually a metal wall painted a matte white. As they approached, it began to rise, revealing the cavern behind it.

"Welcome to Wunderland," Eduardo said.

CHAPTER 9

WUNDERLAND WAS A series of manmade caverns and tunnels carved into the andesite rock of the volcano. Scatters of crystals winked from dark gray stone, reflecting the overhead lights. A petite blond woman named Marisol took the squad off Eduardo's hands and escorted them through the complex, which seemed to be mostly living quarters, laboratories, and little else.

"We get our power from the volcano," Marisol explained.

"It's active, you mean?" Thomas said.

"Yes, although we don't expect a major eruption anytime soon. It blew out a little ash back in the 1960s, I think. I like to hike in the caldera. It's warm enough you don't have to wear a coat, some days."

"That sounds great," Amar said. "Do you also enjoy surfing on tsunamis?"

"We'll have plenty of warning before it erupts," she

assured them. "Ah, here we are."

They had entered a largish round room filled with banks of screens and controls. Most of them were dark, but about half of them seemed to be showing real-time images of the New Cities. Others had various projections of global maps depicting patterns, some constantly shifting, some relatively stable. They might have been network maps of some sort.

"So," someone said. "Dr. Shen has finally come up for air."

The speaker was a woman in perhaps her sixties, her auburn hair shot with silver.

"Dr. Vahlen," Sam said. "So nice to meet you in person."

"The pleasure is mine," she replied.

The name wouldn't have meant anything to Amar a month ago, but that was before he had spent three weeks reviewing XCOM history and tactics. Just as Shen had been the chief engineer of the organization, Vahlen had been the top scientist. Like the rest of the XCOM leadership, she had been presumed dead. But here she was, tunneled into a volcano in the South Atlantic. That, like the building of the Elpis, couldn't have been too cheap. This was starting to feel bigger and bigger.

"I suppose it was too much to ask the old man to come here himself," she said.

"He wanted to," Sam said. "I managed to talk him out of it."

She studied Sam with a slight air of distaste. "I see," she finally said. "Well, his communications were quite the tease. I have been quite agitated, not knowing what you have discovered, what brings you here to me. So sit down; tell me why you've come all this way and what I can do for you."

She ushered them to a round table. One of her assistants brought glasses and a pitcher of water as Sam explained about the downed spaceship. Amar noticed that Lena didn't seem all that surprised—although she had been left out of the initial conversation, after three weeks in a tin can it was hard for anything so big to remain secret.

Vahlen listened patiently, nodding now and then but otherwise not showing much of what was going on behind her gray eyes.

When Sam concluded speaking, she nodded again and tapped the table with her finger, then rose and began slowly strolling about the room.

"It's very odd," she said. "Dr. Shen was always quite . . . Well, I won't say timid . . . but rather *conservative* in his outlook. This plan of his is bold, perhaps even reckless. I wonder what has changed him so."

"I think the war shifted his perspective," Sam said. "And I think Lily—"

"His daughter is with him?" she interrupted, seeming surprised. "That would make a difference, I suppose. He's very lucky to have found her. But she must be an adult now."

"Yes," Sam said. "She is. And she's Dr. Shen's primary assistant."

Vahlen was silent for a moment before continuing, and when she did, it was on an entirely different subject.

"We have not been idle here," she said. "I've been

studying their technology as best I can, from what scraps of it come to me, and by monitoring their communications, their movements, the locations of their power nexuses. I have a great deal of information about their aircraft, which has been languishing to no purpose. It was always our relationship, you know, that I would dream of things and he would build them. Usually these things were a little less than what I conceived of, but he was competent. I would be more than pleased to analyze the data you've brought, Sam, and to make copies of everything relevant I've collected over the years."

She leaned forward and became a little more intense. "But there is something I want in trade. Come with me, please."

She led them down through the maze of tunnels until they reached another room, which held a great deal of equipment that Amar did not recognize, and a few bits he did, such as the autopsy table. And as he turned his gaze around the room, he began to notice other things—like the large cylinders filled with some sort of liquid—and the body parts in them. Most were unrecognizable. Some looked alien, and a few human.

"My location has kept me secure," she said. "Most of what I have learned about their technology I've learned remotely. But it has been difficult to acquire specimens. Shen wants his ship, and yes, I will help with that. But you understand, this war will not be won with machines. It is their biotech we must master—and surpass."

She led them to a wall with a bank of large drawers, like those Amar had once seen in a morgue. She selected one and pulled it open.

"Here," she said.

Amar's first instinct was to reach for his sidearm—but then he saw the thing wasn't moving and was enclosed in what looked like glass, although it was glowing faintly green.

"Is it dead?" Thomas asked.

"Cryosleep," Vahlen said. "I prefer live specimens. So much more can be learned."

Her tone of voice was clinical, but there was something in her expression that suggested something more passionate.

Amar studied the thing. Like the ADVENT soldiers, it had a certain amount of humanity in its appearance—but less. The proportions weren't quite right: Its arms and legs were too long, its head a little too big, and its eyes even larger.

"Bloody hell," he breathed.

"Quite striking, isn't it?" Vahlen said. "All life on Earth is built from the same genetic code. Under such circumstances, genetic manipulation is relatively easy—genes from a tomato can easily be spliced, for instance, into a human genome. But the aliens have a radically different code—or codes, rather. Sectoids and Chryssalids, for instance, are from very different places, genetically—and probably cosmographically. And yet they've somehow made these incompatible systems work together to create something new. What you see here is a human-alien hybrid."

"Like the ADVENT soldiers," Thomas said.

"Precisely. But this specimen has been preserved here for ten years. From what I can make out from their propaganda, they now seem much more human. They're making progress. But toward what? For what reason?

These are the questions we should be asking."

She slid the drawer shut. "Tell Shen I need more specimens, alive if possible. That is what I require if I render him my . . . machine knowledge." She studied their faces as if to make certain they understood.

"I'm sure we can work something out," Sam said.

"Of course," Vahlen replied. Her eyes narrowed a bit. "There is another thing," she said. "This so-called 'contagion.' What do you know of it?"

"Not much, I'm afraid," Sam said. "I've wondered if it's not just part of their propaganda."

"Have you?" Vahlen said. A faint smile appeared on her face, almost a smirk. "I see. Well, if you learn otherwise, I would be interested in what you find. In the meantime, please avail yourselves of my hospitality. Perhaps you would enjoy a hike in the caldera? It's lovely this time of year."

As they began to stand, she looked them over again.

"Which of you is Lena Bishop?" she asked.

"I am," Lena volunteered.

"A moment with you alone, please?"

* * *

Amar opted not to walk in the volcano. One of the staff members invited him to view their substantial library of preinvasion movies and television shows, and he decided that was probably a good use of his downtime. Chitto sat with him for a while but seemed to be mostly bored, and left after an hour or two.

Lena replaced her an hour later. "I've never seen this," she said after a moment, watching a situation comedy about people who worked together.

"You're not allowed to," he said. "They don't want anyone to be reminded of what things were like before they showed up."

She nodded but didn't say anything.

"What did the old lady want with you?" he asked.

"She offered me a job," Lena replied in an odd tone.

"Really?" he said, turning down the volume and facing her. "Doing what?"

"I'll be trained to do something," she said.

"Something? That's awfully vague."

He had been feeling pretty good, but suddenly things felt a little out of control again. He'd assumed that Lena would continue her training as a soldier. While he didn't feel terribly good about that, it meant she would be around. He wanted her around.

"I thought so, too," she said. "Apparently the main thing isn't what job I do but that I remain here."

His mouth felt suddenly a little dry.

"Why?" But he knew the answer. He should have guessed.

She smiled, but it didn't read as happy. Quite the opposite. "Sam warned me that if I came with you I would know too much for them to let me go. It seems he was right. They want me tucked away here, where there's no risk of me jumping ship whenever the Elpis comes to port."

"Vahlen said that?"

"Of course not," she replied, "but I can read between the lines."

"I can talk to Shen," he said. He should have already. How had he not seen this coming?

She shook her head. "It's okay. It's probably for the best. I don't think I could go back home anyway, knowing what I know. But I don't know that I belong on the Elpis— Thomas will never let me have a weapon, and even if she did, I don't know that I'm cut out to do what you do." She gave him a thin smile. "Who knows, maybe after a while I can build a little trust here. Do something useful. Find my mother, or at least the truth about what happened to her."

"Is that really how you feel?"

"I don't know," she said. "I'm trying to put the best face on things, since I don't really have a choice."

Amar nodded, but he wasn't sure what to say.

"There is one tiny little bright side," she said. "Maybe."

"What's that?"

"I'm not going to be in a squad with you."

It caught him off guard, although he knew it shouldn't have. He didn't know who started to lean in first, and he didn't care. Her lips were warm and soft, and in fact everything about her was abruptly completely amazing. And he knew that he shouldn't, that it was stupid, that when they sailed away and left her there it would leave a hole in his chest as sure as any mag rifle could drill. He didn't care. He'd spent years regretting the past and worrying about the future. To be in a moment, this moment, with her, was all he wanted.

He got the call from Thomas an hour later, and it had to

end. That was difficult. He wasn't sure what to say to her, so he just touched his forehead to hers, and they stood that way for a few heartbeats.

"I wonder how long it will take Vahlen to analyze the data," Lena said.

"I don't know," he said. "A few more days. More. I hope."

"Me too," she said. "Find me later, okay?"

"Okay."

* * *

Amar ended up getting his walk in the caldera after all. Thomas sent Toby and him up to patrol and check on some sensors for Vahlen. As promised, the mouth of the volcano was warmer than the rest of the island, so Toby eschewed his hood and instead wore his customary skullcap. He had several—this one was colorful—red, gold and green. It looked new, and Amar wondered if Toby had crocheted it on the Elpis. He usually wore black or brown.

The view down was better than the one from the beach. There was another island of about the same size as the one they were on three kilometers or so away, and beyond that nothing but marine horizon.

But they were fortunate enough to see the sun rise. Amar had always loved the anticipation as the sky grew brighter until the moment when the first fiery little slice of the sun appeared, spilling a golden river across the waves. He was still amazed by how suddenly the sphere appeared, how quickly it leapt from the horizon and then seemed to slow and settle into a statelier pace. It was like a magic trick, distorting one's sense of space and time.

Toby watched with him, looking thoughtful.

"You're a sunrise guy, aren't you?" Toby said.

"I like them, I guess," he said.

"That's not what I mean," Toby said. "I grew up by the water, like you, in Israel and later California. So I never saw the sun come out of the sea like that. I always saw it go into it, vanish, disappear."

"Okay," Amar said. "I've seen that, too."

"But you weren't formed by it," Toby said. "You grew up on the east coast of Malaysia, yes? How old were you before you saw the sun set into the sea?"

"I don't know. When I was seventeen, I guess," he said.

"Right!" Toby said. "I was older than that before I saw what we just watched. You're a sunrise guy. I'm a sunset guy."

"Is there really a difference?" Amar asked, wondering where the lean sniper was going with all of this.

"I don't know," Toby admitted. "I feel like there must be. To see birth every morning, instead of death. That must make a difference."

"Okay," Amar said, "now you're getting all metaphorical on me. What's gotten into you?"

Toby shook his head. "I don't know," he said. "Probably nothing. Too much time to think, I suppose."

He looked off into the far distance, leaving Amar feeling a little awkward. "You know," Amar said, "If you grew up on a little island like this, you would see both events every day. I wonder what that would make you."

Toby smiled. "Then you would get to choose," he said.

Amar's earpiece crackled. It was Thomas.

"You two need to get back here," she said. "Now."

* * *

They met with Vahlen in the same round room. She was clearly angry, reading data from one of her screens and ranting in what sounded like German.

"The signal," she said to her assistant. "It's all wrong. Not at all typical."

She looked at them as they entered. "What have you done?" she demanded.

"I don't understand the question," Thomas replied.

Vahlen stabbed her finger toward one of the screens. It showed six small dots, moving in formation.

"ADVENT troop transports," she said. "Coming here. There can be no mistake."

"Are you saying we were followed?" Thomas said.

"I'm saying nothing of the kind," Vahlen snapped. "If they had followed the Elpis, they would have arrived here just after you did. And they would not be coming from South America. No, they were summoned. My instruments didn't pick up the signal. It was too subtle until I suspected it." She glanced down at the readings, then back at them.

"The signal originates here," she said, waving at her machines. "Something has hijacked my own system and is forcing it to transmit. I've shut it down, of course, but it's already too late."

She handed a small briefcase to Sam. "Get this to Shen,"

she said. "And hurry, you don't have much time before they arrive."

"What about you?" Sam asked. "We need you, Dr. Vahlen. Come with us."

"I am not without defenses," she said. "And I can't leave all of this for them to find. Go! Take the vehicles in the hangar."

As they started out, Amar noticed Lena stood as if rooted. Looking at him. Looking stricken. Vahlen had already turned away, poking furiously at a keyboard.

Between the space of one breath and another, he made his decision.

He grabbed her by the wrist.

"Come on," he whispered. "She's not thinking about you right now. In a minute she may remember."

* * *

"What the hell?" DeLao shouted, as Amar pushed Lena into the jeep and took the wheel. "We can't bring her. She's the one that signaled them; you know it was."

"We don't know any such thing," Amar replied. "Vahlen said it was her own equipment. Get in, and let's get out of here."

"If we take her back to ship, they'll track us there, too," Toby said. "DeLao's right. Nothing else makes sense."

"It wasn't me," Lena said. "I swear it."

The other jeep with Thomas, Sam, Nishimura, and Palepoi was starting to move out.

"We should go," Chitto said.

"Get in, DeLao," Amar said.

"You're a great actor," DeLao told Lena. "I remember when we first picked you up. Pretending you wanted to join us, then turning a gun on us. You're not going to fool us again. Or me, anyway."

Amar started the car and stepped on the gas. With a yelp, DeLao flung himself in.

"You damn fool!" Toby said.

"We've got no time for this," Amar said. "We'll figure it out at the ship."

They made it nearly halfway back before they saw the transports, flying in from the west. For one heart-stopping moment, Amar thought they were fine, that they hadn't been noticed. But then one of the fliers peeled off from the rest.

"You see?" DeLao bellowed.

"Just shut up," Amar said.

Thomas's voice crackled in his ear.

"Stop and get out," she said. "We can't lead them back to the Elpis. We'll fight them here."

The beach offered no cover whatsoever unless you counted the jeeps, which in Amar's experience never lasted long against alien weapons — and in fact tended to turn into bombs. So their only recourse was the mountain behind them. Where ice didn't cover the stone, Amar could see the shape of how the lava had come down in viscous, almost ropey flows with grooves between them that offered some cover. Amar found a likely place a few meters up the slope and took a position, with Chitto on his left flank and DeLao off to his right. Thomas was yet farther to the right, and Sam was with her. The new guy, Palepoi, was a little higher up, behind them. Toby was still spidering his way up the mountain to what looked like a deeper crack in the ice. Nishimura he did not see at all.

Lena was still with him.

"I swear," she said. "I had nothing to do with this."

"Just stay down," he said. "No matter what."

The slope was far too steep for the transport to land on, so the jabbers would have to land on the shingle where they had abandoned their vehicles. Amar watched the craft settle, trying to calm himself.

"This is going to be so much fun," Toby's voice crackled in his ear.

CHAPTER 10

THE HATCH OF the transport opened, and ADVENT soldiers poured out, twelve of them, most running toward their positions. One—a captain—hung back, taking cover behind one of the jeeps. Two shield bearers stood near him and began laying down suppressing fire. Ferromagnetic slugs spalled stone and hissed into the snow all around them.

High above, Amar heard the crack of Toby's high-powered rifle and saw one of the troopers stagger. Amar immediately lifted a bit and unloaded a few rounds on her. Enemy fire spattered against the lava flow in front of him. Everyone else was shooting now. He took aim and fired at the stun lancer trying to come around on his left, but the fellow ducked nimbly behind a burr of stone.

The air was alive with deadly hail, and the sharp scent of ozone nearly overpowered the stink of guano.

"Right there!" Chitto yelped and blasted away. Concentrating on the flanking trooper, Amar had missed the one coming straight toward them, arms flailing. He turned and fired almost point blank at the jabber as it lifted its lance to hit him. It poised over him for a moment, rocking on the balls of its feet as it tried to keep balanced. Amar shot it again, and it went jangling down the slope.

"Bloody hell," he muttered, turning back. Was the other jabber still behind the same rock, or . . . ?

No. It appeared farther upslope, coming almost from behind him. He lifted up to get a shot at it, but the cover fire from the shield bearers forced him back down.

Cursing silently, he waited.

Then, suddenly, the stun trooper was there, leaping forward . . .

No, falling.

"Nice shot, Toby," he said.

"Thanks," Toby said. "I. . . Oh, crap. Guys, they're coming from behind us. Must have landed another transport in the caldera. I can't hold this position."

"Come on down, Toby," Thomas said. "Everybody else get ready. We're going to do a Custer. Palepoi, open the front door. Amar, Chitto—mind the house. DeLao, you're with me."

Amar heard the rocket launcher fire, and then one of the shield bearers exploded in a billowing black cloud. To his right, Thomas bolted down the mountain, her assault rifle yammering.

Amar stood and began firing at the troopers as they emerged from the smoke. A rifle fired, just behind him, and heard Toby whoop.

"Got the captain," he said. Then he made a peculiar

coughing sound. Amar couldn't turn around, but a few seconds later the sharpshooter came staggering by him, his eyes wide and glazed.

"Toby, get down!" he shouted.

Toby looked at him, puzzled, as if he didn't understand what he was saying. Then, a sleet of mag pellets fell on them from above. Toby's armor was shredded, and he tumbled down the slope.

Amar would be just as exposed in a few seconds.

"Lena," he said, trying to keep his voice steady, to not let the panic seep into it. "Get over there with Chitto. Do it now."

He raised and fired upslope as Lena tripped her way across the rough stone. Then he scrambled a little farther up, where a boulder offered some protection. He'd thought his knee was better, but it was aching again, and although his face was cold, inside of his bodysuit he was sweating.

He could only hope Thomas and DeLao were keeping the troopers behind him on the beach busy, because his back was now fully available to them.

They weren't, or at least not entirely. Slugs traced crimson trails up the slope less than a meter from him. There wasn't anything he could do about it, though, so he gritted his teeth and charged for the boulder, waiting for the burst he would never hear, maybe never even feel.

It didn't come. Instead, he heard a rifle fire. He reached the boulder and looked back down. Chitto had Toby's gun. As he watched, she calmly took aim at the remaining shield bearer and put a bullet right between its eyes. Then she shifted her aim to a trooper who had Thomas pinned down behind a jeep.

She squeezed the trigger, and it, too, dropped.

Then Lena stood up, lifting Chitto's shotgun, pointing it at him. He froze, unable to move, unable to believe what she was doing.

Then the muzzle lifted farther, and she fired.

A nightmare came tumbling over him.

His brain told him it was a spider, a spider that stood as high as a man, a spider with knives for legs and a centipede for a face. It hadn't been able to dodge Lena's blast, but it had tried, and it hit the rocks two meters from Lena and Chitto.

He knew he was screaming inarticulately, and he didn't care. He opened up on the monster and turned it into a twitching mass of horribleness.

He looked back up and saw three more of the things bounding toward them with unnatural speed.

Chryssalids. One of the nastier aliens, nearly mindless but incredibly dangerous.

"Let's go!" he hollered. "Now."

As they scrambled down, he saw Nishimura beheading a jabber with her sword. Thomas and DeLao were firing at the enemies coming down the hill, and they hauled ass toward the transports. He signaled for Chitto to go left, and he took right. A glance over his shoulder showed one of the monsters bounding toward him, and he knew he would never make it to cover.

Thomas stood from behind the jeep and fired a burst at the thing, jolting it so it lost its rhythm. But then it scrambled back up. Amar dove past the chief, hoping to get behind the transport. He rolled and turned, expecting the Chryssalid to be right on top of him. But it had changed targets.

As he watched it leap over the jeep, he had what seemed like a long moment to clearly see its four scythe-like legs and two spindly arms ending in four wicked claws, all coming down on Thomas.

Amar saw blood spray as Thomas fired a final burst, and the Chryssalid plunged its claws into her.

Thomas!

Then it turned its glowing yellow eyes toward him.

He emptied his clip into it. He reloaded, and would have shot it again, but it wasn't moving anymore, so he began looking for another target, his breath coming almost like hiccups, like his lungs had shrunk to the size of thumbs.

Troopers and aliens were swarming down the volcano. There were so many of them that he had trouble choosing which one to target. Worse, he saw another transport coming over the lip of the caldera.

He looked around at his companions. DeLao, grim-faced, changing his clip. Nishimura, her sword sheathed, pistol blazing. Lena, shotgun braced on her shoulder.

And Chitto taking shot after shot, as if she was on a firing range rather than in a battle for her life. Her face was a mask, devoid of emotion.

"KB!" Sam yelped from behind him. "Look!"

Where Thomas lay dead, something moved. He watched as the Chryssalid was pushed away, and Thomas staggered to her feet.

"Chief!" he said. "I thought . . ." Then he trailed off, remembering what he knew about the venom Chryssalids carried in their claws.

It should have been obvious, anyway: Thomas had gaping wounds, and her throat was torn out. There was nothing human about her eyes. Like Rider, there was no soul there anymore. No human soul, anyway.

Thomas took a step toward him.

He shot her, again and again, until he was sure she wouldn't get up again. Each bullet seemed to take something of him with it, hollowing him out.

"What are we going to do?" DeLao shouted. "We don't have a chance."

Amar glanced around, suddenly feeling weirdly calm. The penguins that had carpeted the beach earlier were all waddling to the ocean, which was only about two meters behind them.

"Sam," Amar said, "make a break for the water, now. Maybe they won't notice you amongst all the birds. It'll be cold, but you might make it back to the Elpis. It's a chance."

"I can't—"

"Go!" Amar barked. "You're no help to us here."

Sam stared at him, then nodded.

"I'll make it," he said.

"The rest of you, tighten up. Stay behind the transports. Target the Chryssalids first. If anyone has a grenade left, wait until they come in groups. That's going to be soon."

He watched the other transport come, wondering where it would land.

And then, without any warning, the mountain exploded.

In the first insane moment, he thought the volcano had chosen that moment to erupt, but—flash frozen in his mind—he saw a string of explosions too regular to be natural, hurling a thousand canisters skyward . . .

"Into the water, now!" he yelled.

As he turned to run, the canisters opened into blossoms of liquid flame. He saw the flying transport turning end over end, engulfed.

The concussion slammed him face first into the brine, which was only waist deep at that point, but the bottom fell off quickly. He struggled to stay under, let the armor drag him down, as the bitter chill of the water stung his face.

But then he felt blistering heat on his back and swam as best he could, trying to outrun the flame that was spreading on the surface.

He came up for air and saw fire curling all around him. He took one hot breath and sank down again, pulling himself along the rocks on the bottom.

The next time he surfaced, he was clear of the flames. The whole face of the mountain and most of the beach were burning like a torch.

Without their thermal suits, they would have all been dead within minutes. Once clear of the flames, they tried to keep their hands and heads above water to avoid frostbite, but Amar was shivering almost uncontrollably by the time they finally found a bit of beach that wasn't on fire.

They huddled there, warmed by burning propellant and choking on fumes until the flames finally subsided.

Aside from themselves, nothing on the island was moving.

Amar wearily counted heads. They had lost Thomas and Toby, DeLao's arm was half shot off, and Palepoi was wounded in the thigh. Statistically, not bad, but Thomas?

Toby? To lose them was staggering.

It was like his past was being erased. Thomas had recruited him.

But he couldn't get bogged down in that now.

"We're still alive," Amar told the others. "We still have work to do. Drag yourselves up, and let's get back to the Elpis."

DeLao groaned but pulled himself to his feet, and they started toward the ship.

Amar glanced over at Chitto.

"Why the hell haven't you been using a rifle all along?" he asked.

She shrugged. "When I signed up, they gave me a shotgun."

* * *

When they reached the landing, they found Sam standing there. He looked up wearily.

"Thank god," he said. "I thought I was alone."

"What about the Elpis?" Amar asked.

Sam shook his head. "I think she left without us," he said.

But Amar was studying the platform, which was now perforated by magnetic rifle fire.

"I don't think they left," Lena said.

She pointed out to sea. A few hundred meters out a patch of flotsam floated, heaving up and down on the swells.

Amar stared at it, feeling numb. Behind him, the fire on the mountain had diminished to a few flickers amongst the rocks. In the sky above, a black cloud stretched southeast for as far as he could see.

"We've got an hour or two before sundown," Amar told them. "If we don't find someplace to camp, we're going to freeze to death."

"I may be okay with that," DeLao said gloomily.

* * *

The only plants on the island were moss and lichens, and most of that was now gone, courtesy of Vahlen's massive mining project. With nothing to make a shelter from, they had to sleep in a pile that night, sharing body heat. The next day they hiked back toward Wunderland.

Thomas and Toby were pretty much cremated, but since they could, they took time to gather their remains and bury them in the talus at the base of the mountain.

The doors to Wunderland had been blown open. The remains of the three ADVENT transports left were just outside, along with a lot of fried troopers and Chryssalids.

Inside, everything had been torched. The labs were still smoldering, and the power was down.

They found a handful of human bodies, but not enough to account for the population of the island. Hopefully, that was good news. Vahlen had avoided detection and capture for two decades. She must have had an escape plan.

They searched the ruins, looking for anything they could use and not finding very much.

"We can melt ice for water," Sam told them that afternoon. "Judging by the number of sea birds, there must be a lot of fish out there. I don't think survival will be a problem, although it won't be fun."

"Can you build a radio?" Amar asked.

Sam ran his fingers through his hair. "Vahlen did a pretty good job with the scorched earth bit," he replied. "I might manage to make something with very limited range, like I did back when you found me. That's not likely to do us much good."

"You're all missing the point," DeLao said. "The aliens sent out six transports full of goons that never came back. You think they'll let that go?"

"He's right," Amar said. "We need to find a hidey hole. If they don't find us, they'll assume we're dead or we left. Vahlen had some way out. Let's find it."

"What about her?" DeLao said, pointing at Lena.

"I didn't have anything to do with all of this," she said. Her face was smudged, and the hair on one side of her head was badly singed. She still had the shotgun in her hands.

Amar wanted to believe her, but even though he had shouted down DeLao earlier, he had his own doubts. She had been cozying up to him from the beginning, hadn't she? First to lull him into letting his guard down so she could make her escape. Had she kissed him to distract him from the obvious truth, that she was a spy in their midst?

But something about that didn't make sense. If she really was an ADVENT plant, why the whole New City girl act? Why actively make them distrust her if her job was to infiltrate them and lead the jabbers to one of their bases?

"Maybe it's not her," Sam said. "Or maybe it is, and she doesn't know it."

"Yeah, or maybe it's you," DeLao said. "What the hell do we know about you?"

"I know him," Palepoi said, sounding a little irritated, his normally placid face set in a frown. "He's been with Dr. Shen for a long time. He's no traitor."

"Or Chitto," DeLao went on. "She's new. Why exactly did you join up, Chitto?"

"To meet real winners like you," she said. "Gotta find a husband somewhere, right?"

"Stop this," Sam said. "DeLao, stop it. Vahlen said something about the signal being wrong, about something using her own instruments to send the homing signal. Wrong how? What was she talking about?"

Something suddenly clicked in Amar's mind.

"Lena's implant," he said.

Everyone turned to look at him.

"The smugglers took it out," Sam said.

"Maybe," Amar said. "But . . . didn't it feel like those guys gave up too easily?"

"Toby dropped two of them in two seconds," DeLao said.

"Right," Amar conceded. "Then they went a few rounds with us and took off. When has that ever happened?"

"We had the drop on them, and they knew it," DeLao countered. "It wasn't worth staying."

"That's how you or I might think," Amar said. "But jabbers usually call for backup and keep fighting. I thought it stank then, but it reeks now."

"Fine," Nishimura said. "You're saying they wanted us to find her."

"Sure," he said. "Maybe they used her as a stalking horse from the beginning. They must have known she was leaving Gulf City and heading out into the settlements. Right, Lena?"

"Of course I told them where I was going," Lena said. "You're supposed to register for travel." A look of horror was slowly spreading across her face.

"Right," Sam said. "So they followed you to Greenville, and when the smugglers drugged you, ADVENT followed them to their depot. Maybe they had already cut your implant out, maybe not. Either way, ADVENT killed them. Then they put in a new implant. A different kind of implant, maybe a more advanced one built for long-range tracking. We showed up, they made it look like a fight, and then they left."

"And they've been tracking us ever since," Lena said. "Oh my god."

"Hang on," DeLao said. "I examined her. Sure they sewed her up, but I checked. There was no implant."

"There's one way to find out," Nishimura said.

"Yes," Lena said. "Yes, do it."

DeLao got his medical kit. He gave Lena a local and then cut through her scar, pulling the wound open and dabbing at it with a cloth to stanch the bleeding.

"See?" he said. "No implant."

Instead of looking at her cut, Lena was staring at Amar.

"Dig a little deeper," he said.

Lena paled further as DeLao cut further into her muscle tissue. After a minute, his eyebrows lifted.

"*Mierda*," he said.

He changed out the scalpel for forceps and after a moment pulled something out. It was tiny, but as he pulled, long red strands as thin as hair came out behind it. Lena closed her eyes and began shaking, but she bore up until almost a half meter of the stuff emerged from her.

"What the hell is that?" Sam asked.

Amar studied the tiny bead from which the hairs protruded.

"If I had to guess, I would say it's biological. Maybe it amped up her nervous system so it could transmit a signal to Vahlen's equipment. It's really a question for Vahlen."

They debated trying to keep the thing for further study, but in the end the risk was too great. DeLao made some notes, and then they burned it and tossed the ashes into the ocean.

CHAPTER 11

NISHIMURA FOUND THE secret escape route, which was no longer quite so secret—the final blast that torched Vahlen's complex had shifted the hidden panel and revealed a corridor and stairs beyond. Locked and loaded, they followed them up and emerged in the gigantic bowl of the caldera.

But what they found was bad news—the hulks of five helicopters, as torched as anything on the beach. They could see a number of charred skeletons that must have been blown clear of the crash.

DeLao sat down, rested his bandaged arm on his knee, and put his head down.

"They didn't make it," Palepoi said, voicing the obvious.

"Yeah," DeLao said. "And now we have no way off of this island."

"Well," Palepoi said. "That's that, isn't it?"

It seemed so to Amar. He wasn't sure how far the nearest inhabited land was, but he was willing to bet it was a long, long way. With luck, they could avoid the next patrol ADVENT sent out, but then what? The base had just been resupplied by the Elpis. How long before another supply ship came?

Was there any other supply ship?

Sam turned slowly toward them, his face stern. His slight body seemed to grow taller.

"No," Sam said. "That is *not* that. We're alive, and we have information the resistance needs. So we do not give up. We hide. We survive. And we do the mission."

"How?" Amar asked.

"You lead your troops," Sam said. "Dig in someplace. Let me worry about the rest."

* * *

Chitto went up to the rim of the caldera with the scoped rifle to watch for fliers while the rest of them went to work on closing up the once-secret door, in hopes of using the upward passage as a hiding place; the crater end of the tunnel could be easily disguised with packed snow.

The problem was, they couldn't shift the thing back. The metal door had warped in the intense heat; it wouldn't slide or be shifted a centimeter in any direction.

"We're just going to have to blow it," Sam finally said. "Collapse the tunnel."

"With grenades?"

"I can make it work," Sam said "I just need to place them right and rig a way to detonate them from a distance. Nishimura, give me a hand."

About an hour later, Sam and Nishimura emerged from the tunnel. Then, a muffled explosion blew a cloud of black dust out of the tunnel mouth. They waited for it to clear and then went cautiously back down to see the results.

"Holy smokes," Sam said, when they arrived. "That is not what I was going for."

The ceiling had indeed collapsed—and so had the floor.

Amar's earphone crackled.

"I see something," Chitto said. "Coming from the west, like last time."

"Okay," Amar said. "This is it. Everyone in. Chitto, get down here, fast."

She did get there fast. She must have more or less skated down the crater wall.

Once she was in, they collapsed the pile of snow and ice they had hacked up. They couldn't make it smooth without leaving someone outside, but it was what it was. If anyone looked really close, they were screwed. They could only hope no one looked really close.

When they were all in the passage, Sam called him back down.

"I think I found something," he said.

* * *

The explosion had opened a second tunnel beneath the first, and in fact the first three meters had been a trap door laminated with stone to make it appear natural. It didn't lead up, but proceeded in a fairly level manner for maybe a hundred meters before widening into a large cavern. Most of it was filled with water, except for a walkway on their side and a floating dock. There was a small cabin cruiser tied up there, but there were six empty slips. The cavern wasn't large enough for the Elpis, but you could fit a couple of decent-sized vessels in there, or seven small ones.

"Son of a bitch," Sam said.

"But what about the helicopters?" Nishimura asked.

"A ruse, obviously," Sam said. "Misdirection."

"But the bodies . . ." DeLao protested.

"Maybe they were dead already," Amar said. "People killed in the attack. Or some of Vahlen's specimens."

"Maybe," Sam said. "It doesn't bear a lot of thinking about. It looks like she did escape, by boat. Like us, she probably figured the ADVENT would think she was dead and call off the search."

And now *they* had a boat. Things were looking up. If the jabbers up there right now didn't find them and kill them all, that is.

He was still thinking that a few minutes later when a series of tremors shook the island.

Sam laughed. "I guess it's a good thing we didn't search through the bodies," he said.

* * *

After twenty-four hours had passed, Nishimura went out to check and reported no sign of ADVENT troops or transports in the area—living ones, anyway. One ruined flier lay on its side in the blast radius that had earlier been wrecked helicopters, along with the bits and pieces of ADVENT soldiers.

That was the good news.

Sam told them the bad news. He had found some charts in the boat.

"We're about 13,000 kilometers from where we need to be," he told them. "That's as the crow flies. And we're not flying. What we have is a smallish boat."

"Where are we going again?" Amar asked.

Sam looked uncomfortable for a moment and then shrugged. "You might as well know. If something happens to me, the rest of you will have to carry on. Our target is in India, in the Western Ghats."

"Wait one moment," Nishimura said, her dark eyebrows crooked around a frown. "I've been looking at the charts, too. This boat has a range of a few hundred kilometers. You're talking about going east. Cape Town is more than 5,000 kilometers away."

"Sure," Sam agreed. "But there are islands between here and there, and some are marked as fuel depots."

"The nearest one I saw marked that way is around 2,500 kilometers," Nishimura said. "Still way too far."

"What do you suggest then?" Sam asked.

"South Georgia Island is a fuel depot, too. The Elpis stopped over there on the way down. It's just under 800 kilometers from here. From there we can hop to the Malvinas and on to South America."

"That's going the wrong direction, though," Sam pointed out.

"*Cojudo!*" Nishimura swore. "Don't you get it? This mission is *done*. That target is out of our reach—and even if we could get there, the Shens are dead. God knows where

151

Vahlen is headed. From the looks of it, she had better ships with longer range than this one. Without them, what are we going to do with a crashed alien ship?"

"I know something about their technology," Sam said. "And I have Vahlen's data. Once we find the ship, we can attract others with the skills we need."

"But we won't make it," Nishimura said.

"There's plenty of fuel," Sam said. "We can drag extra tanks behind us to increase our range."

"And if we meet a storm, we'll go down like so many stones," Nishimura said. "I intend to be of use to this resistance. I don't intend to squander my life in a hopeless attempt to reach *India* from the South Atlantic in a glorified rowboat. When we had the Elpis, sure. Now we're just lucky to be alive. So let's take the information you have to someone who has the capability of using it."

"We can do it," Sam said. "I know we can. And sailing west, the distances are better, but we would still have to take on extra fuel to reach the Malvinas."

"Not nearly as much," Nishimura said. She lifted her chin and wagged a finger at him. "Wait a minute. You ran those numbers, too."

"Yeah," Sam said, "I did."

"But you didn't present going to South America as an option."

Sam sighed. "Is it just me?" he asked. "Is it just me who feels that when I close my eyes and try to sleep, I see Dixon, Sergei, all of those guys, Thomas, Toby, Dr. Shen—every night, more faces. Lily Shen, everyone on the Elpis. This was Shen's dream, Nishimura. People died for this, believing we would carry on, finish, seize the lightning. There's only one boat, and I know you guys can take it if you want to. But if you outvote me and retreat to South America, I won't be with you. I'll bloody swim to India if I have to."

For several long moments, no one spoke. Then Chitto cleared her throat.

"That's pretty dramatic," she said. "A little over the top. But if I can put in my two cents here—I'd kind of like to see India."

"The Ghats are supposed to be beautiful this time of year," Amar said. "And I have some contacts in the area."

Everyone looked at Nishimura, who threw up her hands. "The Andes are nice this time of year, too," she snapped. "But whatever. *Bacán.* India it is." She glared around at them. "So who knows how to sail?"

When no one said anything, Sam raised his hand.

"I found a manual," he said.

* * *

That evening, Amar went back up to the lip of the caldera alone and looked westward, out over the sea.

The sky was unusually clear, and the dark orange ball of the sun was just touching the horizon. He watched it disappear a little bit at a time, thinking about how much more slowly it seemed to happen than the sunrise. The last spark seemed to linger, a tiny ember drowning in the waters. Then, finally, it was gone, leaving the night to the stars.

"Goodbye, Toby," he said.

* * *

Amar dragged himself up to take his watch. It was mid-day, and the seas were rough. Sometimes the horizon was only a few meters away as they descended into a trough; when they reached the top of a swell he could see forever. But there was nothing to see except more water.

The temperature was still close to freezing, although they had been sailing northeast for five days. He—like everyone on board—was starving. They had managed to catch some fish before leaving, and they had some rations in their packs. But they had been a lot less successful at finding food out in the deep water.

What was more alarming was that they were running out of potable water—and, for that matter, fuel. The boat was not, of course, able to access any sort of global positioning system. Sam was sailing with charts, a compass, and an astrolabe. Given that this was his first attempt at such a thing, and that the island they were looking for was little more than a big rock, they might have even passed it a day ago.

South America was starting to sound pretty good, although they were way beyond the point of no return on that score.

He peered over at Lena, in her bunk, still asleep. Neither of them had mentioned what had happened back in Wunderland. At first, there had been too much going on, and now there was no chance for privacy. And although it had seemed like a good thing at the time—no, *had* been a good thing at the time, in that moment—now he wasn't so sure. Like Sam, he kept seeing Thomas and Toby in his dreams—not as he wanted to remember them, but as he had last seen them. He now believed Lena had not been an intentional spy, but it was hard to put aside the fact that if there had never been a Lena—if she had not left her life in Gulf City to pursue a naive, ill-advised adventure—his two friends would still be alive. They would all be on their way to India, not in a tiny ship designed for relatively short voyages, but in the Elpis. He wouldn't be freezing and feeling his gut growing tighter every day. He would have fewer nightmares.

Chitto had seen Thomas die as well, and early in the voyage she had some questions about that. Rather than having to explain it more than once, he'd called a meeting.

"Chitto was wondering why I shot Thomas after the Chryssalid attacked. Does anyone know?"

"I've heard about it," DeLao allowed. "I'm glad I didn't see it."

"I've seen it happen," Nishimura said. "In Tabasco."

"Yeah, me too," Amar said. "Two months in under Thomas, near Jakarta."

"That's real nice," Chitto said. "But I don't know what you're talking about."

Amar clasped his hands together. "There is a sort of wasp that injects its eggs into a species of orb spider. The pupae grow inside of the spider, eating away. Toward the end, the spider suddenly starts weaving webs of a kind it never has before, because the pupae have taken control of its nervous system and are forcing the spider to build a web to protect them when they've finally eaten their way out. There's another wasp that injects eggs into a ladybug, and when the larvae come out for cocoons, a virus that also came from the wasp forces the ladybug to stay there and stand guard over the babies. In effect, they turn their hosts into zombies.

"Chryssalids do something like this, but with humans, and they do it fast. The Captain Thomas who stood up wasn't Captain Thomas anymore. And in another few minutes, a brand new Chryssalid would have clawed its way out of her. So if you can, you don't let that happen. If one of those things takes your buddy down, the best thing you can do is shoot her."

Never mind that he still felt sick every time he thought of that moment, of seeing his rounds strike the Chief. It had felt like murder, and to part of him it still did.

But he didn't tell them that.

That had been on day one. Now, on day five, nobody wanted to talk about much at all. Chitto and DeLao were seasick a lot of the time. Amar usually felt okay on deck but not as well below if seas were high.

He had spent his share of time on the water—in the South China Sea, the Sulu Sea, a bit in the Indian Ocean. But that had mostly been going from mainland to island to island, never that far from land. They had crossed the Pacific stowed away on an automated container ship the size of a small city, and the weather had been tropical to fair. Not until now had he understood how bleak and utterly empty a place like the ocean could be.

CHAPTER 12

WHEN HE FIRST saw Gough Island on the horizon, it looked like a jewel. The sky was clear, unlike their last stop, and it wasn't covered in snow, but instead shone like an emerald beacon. As they drew nearer, he saw that it was equally treeless, however, its color the result of moss and lichen and maybe a few scrubby bushes. But it was land, and fuel, and hopefully food. They navigated toward where the map claimed the depot was.

As they drew near, Chitto spotted something rising from the shoreline. Amar's heart sank. It wasn't a transport. Transports weren't armed. This was one of the ADVENT's smaller gunships.

"Well, that was totally worth it," Nishimura said.

Chitto started firing at the edge of her range. Amar didn't pin a whole lot of hope on that. She might be a crack shot, but these things were thick-skinned. Maybe if Palepoi could hit it just right with his last rocket . . .

A red line appeared between their boat and the flier, and the impact hurled them all from their feet. Palepoi toppled overboard, and the boat listed as it started taking on water.

"They hulled us below the water line," Amar shouted. "They could have vaporized us with a missile. They may be trying to take us alive. Don't make it easy for them." He raised his weapon but waited. He only had one clip left and wanted to make it count.

He saw Lena looking at him, and he tried to smile. He wished that they had been able to talk, that he had been able to touch her face again.

Don't get sloppy, he told himself.

The flier suddenly jerked and spun half-around, a gout of black smoke curling up from it. An instant later, Amar heard the detonation. Then the craft erupted in green and yellow flame, spinning crazily as it sank seaward. It struck the water, stood up on its end, and then hit flat. The water around it began to boil, and just as it vanished from view, seawater rose in a half sphere ten meters high. A moment later, the shock hit them and lifted their little boat, but they were already so heavy from being half-sunken that they didn't capsize.

Beyond, nearer the island, Amar saw two puffs of smoke drifting off in the wind, revealing the Elpis.

* * *

Dr. Shen looked somehow frailer than when Amar had last seen him, although it had only been a matter of days. But for Amar those days had seemed more like months, and perhaps it had been the same for Shen. In fact, everyone seemed to be affected, so maybe it was because it had been laid bare how precarious their enterprise was, how slim their chances of success. There was the inevitable debriefing, and condolences for Thomas and Toby. And explanations from Captain Laaksonen. After greeting them, Lily Shen insisted her father retire. He'd apparently risen from his sick bed to see them come aboard.

"The first patrol dropped depth charges on us," Captain Laaksonen explained. "We released countermeasures—basically assorted junk, which is what you probably saw on the surface. We did sustain damage, however, and Dr. Shen was injured in a fall. That left me in charge, so the decision to leave was mine. It seemed impossible that anyone had survived the fire, and I felt I had to put the Shens and our mission before all else. When we got word that a second strike force was on the way, I believed we should be as far from that place as possible."

He looked a bit uncomfortable, which was out of character for Laaksonen. "I deeply underestimated your resourcefulness," he said. "Fortunate that you chose the same destination that we did."

"It was really the only choice if we were to carry out the mission," Amar said. "Sam saw that clearly. The rest of us had to be persuaded."

"You could have abandoned the mission," Laaksonen replied. "You did not, and for that I salute you." He quickly changed the subject, bringing a map up on the conference room screen. "The ADVENT put a relatively large amount of resources into trying to find us," he explained. "The craft we just shot down arrived here sometime before we did. We were submerged, but we couldn't leave because we needed to refuel—we had planned to do that on Vahlen's island. As you probably know, the next fuel depot is thousands of kilometers away. In another day, we would have been forced to surface. Fortunately you arrived in time to distract them."

He traced a rough circle around Vahlen's island.

"We believe they staked out every rock and atoll within about 2,500 kilometers of here. It is good news that Vahlen escaped, but I fear she may not be safe. Nor can we worry about that. Our task is to vanish again. We will depart as soon as we refuel and resupply, hopefully within the next ten hours. Then we will push on. If you need shore leave, take it now."

* * *

After nearly a week on a rickety craft, and not knowing when he would be able to set foot on land again, Amar decided a hike was worth doing. The fuel depot was near an old weather station on the southeast end of the island. Two rather dramatic peaks rose farther north, but they were too far away, so he settled on a nearby rise that would afford him a better view.

When he reached the summit, he was a little disappointed to find that Sam had had the same idea. It wasn't just the view Amar was after, but a little precious solitude.

"Reminds me a lot of Scotland," Sam told him. "Especially the Isle of Skye. Except for the penguins."

Amar had noticed a few penguins. These had funny

little sprays of yellow feathers that looked almost like hair, and they weren't in anything like the same numbers as their less showy cousins back on Vahlen's island. Dozens of other bird species abounded, and what looked like seals sunned on the narrow beach below them.

"How long since you've been home?" Amar asked.

"If you mean the town I was from," Sam said, "it doesn't exist anymore. If you mean Scotland, I haven't been there since I was eleven. That's when Dr. Shen took me on the Elpis as a favor to my father. I've been there pretty much since then."

"Is Dr. Shen okay?"

Sam pursed his lips.

"The Elpis apparently took a pretty hard hit, and everyone inside got shaken up pretty good. He's got a concussion and a cracked fibula, all that on top of some more persistent health problems. But he's determined to find this ship. He really believes it will be the turning point for the resistance. For XCOM."

"Do you?" Amar asked.

Sam shrugged. "I don't know if will be a turning point so much as a start. We still have a long way to go and a lot to do, even after we find the ship." He glanced off to the sea. "I appreciate your support back there on Vahlen's island," he said. "Without you weighing in, I think it wouldn't have gone my way."

"I was trying to think what Thomas would have done," Amar said. "I think I got it right."

"Those are big shoes to fill," Sam said, "but I think you're up to it."

For a moment, he didn't even know what Sam was talking about. Then it sank in.

"What?" Amar said. "No. I'm not a squad leader."

"Who is, then?" Sam asked. "You stepped up when Thomas died. Anybody could have, but you were the one. DeLao is as experienced as you are, and Nishimura is more so. But you took command and nobody questioned it."

"All I remember is telling everybody to get in the water," Amar said.

"Maybe that's how it started," Sam pointed out. "But now you're in charge, trust me."

"I don't know that I want to be," Amar said. He remembered what Thomas had told him, back on the Elpis.

"If I know you like I think I do," Sam said, "you don't have a choice." He stood up. "I'll make a little room," he said, and began walking down the other side of the hill.

Amar wondered at first what he meant, but then he saw Lena approaching from the depot.

"Hey, no," Amar said. "It's not like that."

"Look," Sam said, "don't be a jackass." He continued on down the slope.

"Would you rather be alone?" Lena asked when she arrived, brushing a stray brown hair from her face. Her New City hairstyle was becoming not only longer, but more unruly. She looked entirely beautiful.

"No," he said.

She looked a little relieved. "We haven't . . ." she began, then stopped, looking embarrassed. "We haven't really had a chance to talk."

"Right," he said.

"Don't you think we should?"

He'd tried to get his thoughts on this together. He thought he had, but suddenly he didn't know what to say.

"I really wanted that," he finally managed. "To kiss you. I want to now."

"Why don't you then?"

"It distracted me," he told her.

She smiled. "I should hope so," she said.

"No. I mean that you put me off my game. I should have realized immediately that they found us through you. I should have left you with Vahlen. You would have been safe with her. Then I wouldn't have had to argue with DeLao, which slowed us down. I wouldn't have been worried about you during the firefight. Thomas might still be alive."

"You wish you had left me with Vahlen?" she asked.

"No," he said. "What I'm saying is that deep down I knew I should have left you there, for all kinds of reasons. But what I wanted was for you to be with me. And that's what I acted on."

"But that's what I wanted, too," she said. "And I know we're not exactly even, but I think I saved your life."

"Without doubt," he said. "That's part of the problem."

"That I distract you? Put you off your game?" she asked, her face beginning to flush. "Maybe in another life?" she went on, hurling his words back at him. "Is that what you're telling me? If we had met on a dance floor rather than downrange?"

"Yes," he said. "I guess it is."

"Let me clue you in about something," Lena said,

stepping closer. "There *is* no other life. This is it. And do you really think that just because we're not actively making out it's going to change how you feel? That you'll be any less 'off your game'? Because I sure as hell know I don't feel that way."

A little tear began trickling down her face, but her expression was fiercer than anything. He reached to brush the tear, but she stopped him by grabbing his hand.

This is not happening, he thought.

But of course it was, and for a while on that hill overlooking the sea, nothing else seemed to matter but her, and time ceased to pass.

* * *

The Elpis set out in the early afternoon, and Amar watched the last land he would see for almost a month retreat into the distance and then memory. The prospect of being spotted by another ADVENT flier weighed heavily on them, but without the chip to track them, and presumably having no idea where they were going, the search zone would now spread in a circumference with Gough Island at its center. That made the first few days crucial, and they submerged at any slight indication of something passing nearby.

In a few days, however, with more than a thousand kilometers of open sea between them and the depot, they began to breathe easier. Still, they steered farther south of the tip of South Africa than was likely necessary, and when they put in to refuel at a secluded bay on the coast of Madagascar, Amar used it as a live ammo training session, even though every sensor they had — and the inhabitants of the depot — said there was nothing to worry about.

It turned out, mercifully, that there wasn't, but it gave the greener troops a chance to learn to maneuver on land rather than on the upper deck of a submersible.

Once everything was secure, it also gave him more time to be alone with Lena, which pretty much never happened on the ship. Even though everyone seemed to know something was going on with them, it still seemed like a bad idea to be obvious about it. She had backed out of the military training, which was a relief, because it reduced his qualms about their relationship. Sam, as it turned out, was right. Everyone seemed to think of him as Thomas's successor, and he was settling into the part. Being Lena's commanding officer would be very much a conflict of interest.

Lena began working with Lily Shen instead. She was apparently a quick study, even though her background in science and mathematics was pretty minimal. The ADVENT administration had very little interest in educating the populations of their cities beyond a minimum — and highly propagandized — curriculum.

"Or as Lily puts it," Lena told him, as they walked along the beach, hand in hand, "technology is something humans don't have to worry their pretty little heads about. ADVENT will take care of all of that technical stuff, don't you worry."

"That sounds like her," Amar said. "Does it jibe with your experience?"

"Yes, actually," she said. "But growing up that way, it doesn't seem like a bad thing. You don't have to understand biology to breathe, so why should you learn how a media screen does what it does?"

"No, I get it," he said. "I don't know much about the stuff either. I couldn't have built a radio, like Sam did."

"Well, you have other qualities," she said.

"Nice to hear. So what are you helping her with right now?" he asked.

"I'm learning a little about cybernetics," she said.

"Go on."

"It's all very hush-hush," she said. "You may have to torture it out of me."

"I've got training along those lines," he said. "Don't tempt me."

"I believe you do tempt me, sir," she said.

"I don't deny that," he said, leaning in for a kiss.

"Battle droid," she said a few minutes later, when they both got their breath back. "A sort of support robot for you guys."

He thought about that for a moment.

"What?" she asked.

"I just wonder how that will go over," he said.

"What do you mean?"

"Generally, when we run into a robot, it's trying to kill us," he said. "Having one on our side—that might be hard for some to trust."

"Well, it's only in preliminary stages," she said. "Lily is actually going to want to talk to you about the features it ought to have."

"Here's a better idea," he said. "Let's have a general round table on the subject with everybody, or at least the squad leaders. If they're included in the process, they'll more likely be on board with it."

"I'll mention that to her," Lena said. "We have to be back at the ship in an hour. Is there anything you want to do before we go back?"

"I'm doing it," he said.

CHAPTER 13

THE WESTERN GHATS were mountains in the southwest of the Indian subcontinent. The part of the range they were interested in lay in what had once been the state of Kerala. Civilization there was old, and it had formed the hub of the spice trade for millennia. Black pepper, nutmeg, cloves from the distant islands of Maluku all passed through the port at Cochin. Indeed, so important was Kerala that Prince Henry the Navigator of Portugal decided it ought to be conquered, so beginning an era of colonialism that wouldn't end until the twentieth century.

Now Kerala, like the rest of planet Earth, had new colonizers.

Much of the Ghats had always been thinly populated—the population of Kerala had lived mostly along the coast. This was now doubly the case—the Ghats were contagion zones, and strictly off limits. But whereas Kerala had once had an extensive backwater transportation system of inland waters, rivers, and canals, outside of New Kochi, these backwaters had not been maintained, and years of flooding and meandering had taken their toll, turning them into messy, brackish marshes.

Which made them an excellent place to hide the Elpis. The real challenge was finding a place deep enough that the ship would not be revealed at high tide. It took a little patience, but in the end they found such a place.

The plan was for Sam and Amar to lead an expedition to discover if the ship was still there after all these years and in sound enough shape to be worth their time. The elder Dr. Shen was better, but the way was going to be physically demanding, and Sam wanted to delay his journey there until it was deemed necessary. That meant that Lily was going instead, and she was taking Lena as an assistant.

Amar had deeply mixed feelings about this. In his time on board the Elpis, he had come to realize that Lily was not only healthier than her father but also that she was far brighter—and that was saying something. He didn't know what her IQ was, but it had to be off the charts. From their description, a handful of notes, and an examination of Lena, she had not only figured out how the bio-implant worked but also built a detector that would expose that sort of device. Of the two Shens, Lily was the least expendable.

But she was also stubborn, and she outranked him.

(Having Lena in harm's way didn't settle easily on his shoulders either.)

For his people, he chose Chitto, Nishimura, and Dux, who was by that time pretty well mended. DeLao's arm was still stiff. To round things out, he added Chakyar, a young man originally from Dubai. He had some medical training and spoke Malayalam, the predominant language of the area. He was only twenty-three, but he already had a streak of gray in his otherwise black hair and eyes like a summer sky.

They made their way over the crumbling infrastructure to Piravom, a settlement on the outskirts of New Kochi that was supposed to have a resistance cell tucked away in it. When they reached it, they found an ADVENT patrol checking the place, but they soon left.

Pivarom was bigger and more crowded than most of the settlements Amar had experience with. It appeared to go on forever and seemed more convoluted than a human brain. Among the huts and stalls and family-sized tents, a few old architectural gems stood out: Syrian Christian churches that didn't look quite like anything he'd ever seen, a Hindu temple of Shiva. A river separated the settlement into two parts, which had once been connected by a bridge. It bustled with attractive houseboats called *kettuvallam*, adorned with elaborate wicker roofs and walls.

He very soon had cause to celebrate bringing Chakyar along. English had lost much of its currency here. But even with the advantage of a translator, Amar began to think they were getting the runaround. This man said to go see that man, that man to see such-and-such woman. They seemed to be going in circles.

Then they turned a corner and found themselves surrounded by men with knives. One of them, a sharp-featured, clean-shaven fellow in his late forties or early fifties, stepped forward.

"You've been looking for us," he said in English. "Tell me why."

"Don't you want the current passcodes?" Amar asked.

The man gave him a long, searching look. It felt as if the others were drawing nearer.

"We aren't current," the fellow finally said. "Our radio is down."

"If you have the parts," Sam said, "I might be able to fix that."

The man studied them again and then nodded. "We are vulnerable here," he said, "so I must be cautious. You will wear hoods and be conducted to our base. Is that acceptable?"

"It is," Amar said. He had more or less expected it.

* * *

"My name is Valodi," the man said, when they reached their destination and their stifling black hoods were removed. "Welcome to my command."

It appeared to have once been some sort office building, although it had decidedly seen better days. Valodi offered them a seat and had some food brought, some spiced lentils and rice with a little fish.

"I'm sorry if we seem rude," Valodi said. "But we've had to relocate several times this year, and raids have become near constant."

"I understand your caution," Amar said.

"Tell me why you are here," Valodi said.

"We need a guide," Sam said, "into the Ghats. I can show you the place on a map. It would be good, too, if we had some sort of ground transportation."

"That's a lot to ask," Valodi said. "What do you have to offer in return?"

"Well, for starters," Sam said, "I can fix that radio. We also have medicine, ammunition, and so forth. You tell us what you need, and I'll tell you if we have it."

The man nodded. "Medicine we can use, certainly."

"But the most important thing I can offer you is hope," Sam said.

"That is also in short supply," Valodi said. "Can you explain more plainly what you mean?"

"Not yet," Sam said. "Not here. But I promise you, it will be worth it." He smiled. "One more thing I can offer you is of immediate practicality."

He took a small, baton-shaped device from his bag.

"One of our scientists just developed this. We haven't tested it, but it should be able to tell you if someone has been chipped without having to find the scar. Test it, and you can have it. And several more like it."

Valodi took the device and examined it curiously.

"That's easily tested," he said. "Fix our radio, and we can discuss the rest."

* * *

After Sam got the radio working, the Pivaromis warmed to them quickly. The chip detector also worked and was a big hit with them, as they had apparently also once been Trojan-horsed by someone who appeared to have had their chip removed. Valodi assured them that he would guide them into the mountains himself, but the vehicles would take a couple of days to procure. As a sign of good faith, he let them wander the settlement, which of course meant they now knew their way to and from his hideout.

It was toward the end of the southern monsoon season and stifling hot. The rain pounded outside as it had for most of the day and all of the night before. Amar and Sam sat playing cards with three of Valodi's men in a dirty white room with no electric lighting. All of the illumination came through a bank of broken windows and the liquid curtain beyond. A few mosquitos had taken refuge in the room and were doing their best to suck him dry. A tokay gecko the size of a squirrel clung to one corner of the room, croaking now and then.

Amar had been playing for about an hour and was still a little uncertain of the rules, although Sam seemed to be doing fine.

Lena walked into the room.

"What's up?" he asked.

"Lily is getting restless," she said. "There's a power node just outside of town. She wants to get some readings from it. She says it could help her synthesize their energy source."

"That sounds like a very bad idea," he said. "Please ask her to consider not going."

"I second that," Sam said.

"And if she insists?"

He sighed. "Then come back here and get us. We'll assign her a detail."

"I'll tell her," Lena said, "for a kiss."

"Oh, whatever," Sam said. "If that's what it takes."

Lena's look of outrage was probably not entirely affected.

"You threatened to kill me once," she said, "if you don't remember."

"Well, that was, what, a couple of months ago?" Sam said. "Cut me a little slack."

"If you try and kiss me, I'll cut *something*," she said. She said it lightly, but beneath her tone, Amar felt there was still some resentment there. Lena did not forget, and she did not easily forgive.

"I'll take one for the team," Amar said. He stood up and walked her out of the room.

They stood in the darkened hall for a moment. Her gaze searched his, as if trying to find something. Then she stood on her tiptoes and kissed him. It was soft and sweet and seemed to linger well after their lips parted.

"I'll tell her the Chief said to sit tight," she said.

He returned to the game, but his mind was no longer on it. Instead he stared out the window at the rain, the misty encampment, at some children rolling around in the mud, just as he had once. It rained almost every day during monsoon season, and kids got bored.

* * *

An hour later, Lena burst back into the room, soaked, out of breath, and ashen. Her face and arms were covered in small, blood-bright scratches, as if from thorns.

"Lena!" Amar blurted, running over to her. "What happened? What's wrong?"

"I tried," she said. "I tried to talk her out of it, but she insisted."

"Lena," Sam said, "slow down, ease back. What's going on?"

But Amar already knew. Back in the kampung, when he was a kid, families would get together and watch bootleg movies from back before the conquest. Some of them ended badly, and every time he watched them he hoped that this time everything would turn out okay. Of course, it never did. This felt like that to him. As Lena gasped out her story, he let his hands drop from her shoulders and stepped back. He hoped it wouldn't turn out the way he feared, but he knew better.

Lily Shen couldn't be convinced. Lena had tried to talk her out of it at first and then begged her to let her find some soldiers to bring along. Lily had been impatient, arguing that soldiers would only attract attention that a woman alone would not.

Lena didn't know exactly where the power node was, and was afraid if she came looking for help they might lose Lily entirely, so she'd instead chosen to go along with her.

"I thought she was just going to take some readings," Lena said. "But then she opened up a panel and starting fiddling with it. The next thing I knew, an ADVENT patrol showed up. They took Lily."

"Alive?" Sam asked.

"She was alive when they took her," Lena said.

"What about you?" Amar asked. "How did you get away?"

"I ran," she answered. "I was unarmed, and there were four of them. Lily ran, too, but she tripped and fell into a canal. I was already on the other side."

He remembered a joke his uncle used to tell. Two men were running from a bear. One of them said, "It's too fast—we'll never outrun it."

"I don't have to outrun it," the other man said. "I just have to outrun you."

It didn't seem all that funny at the moment.

"You left her there," Amar said.

She stared at him, a look of stark betrayal on her face. "What else was I supposed to do?" she asked. "Would you rather I was taken, too?"

He realized that he had spoken aloud what he had meant to be a private thought, almost never a good thing.

"No," he said. "No, of course not. You're right. Now at least we know what happened. You did the right thing. I'm just trying to wrap my head around this."

But what he was thinking was that Lena should have found a way to stop her.

"I've got mine wrapped," Sam said. "This is a disaster."

"You can say that again, brother," Amar sighed.

Everything had been going great. They were a few days from finding the ship. They had the beginnings of a supply route and the support of the local resistance. And now this.

Lena still looked stricken, but now she also looked a little angry.

"I'm sorry," Lena said. "I wish I could have stopped her."

If wishes were horses, Amar thought.

"It's fine," he lied. "It's going to be okay. This just makes things a little more complicated."

He looked northeast, to where the night sky was tinged

with blue city light. The rain began to come down harder.

"We're going to have to go get her, that's all." He stood up. "I need to talk to Valodi."

* * *

"They didn't kill her outright," Valodi said. They were in his command room, an unassuming space with a small desk and a map drawer. A faded portrait of Mahatma Gandhi was fixed on the wall, slightly crooked. "That's a good sign. Next they'll take her to processing."

"Do you know where that is?"

He nodded. "We've surveilled it but never made any attempt to rescue anyone. If that's what you're planning, it won't be easy."

Valodi had a tendency, Amar found, to understate things. His expression suggested that what he really meant was that it would be nearly impossible.

"That's what I'm planning," Amar said. "Lily is vital to this mission."

"What's so special about her?" Valodi asked.

Amar was weighing whether he should tell him when Sam made the decision for him. "Have you ever heard of Dr. Raymond Shen?" he asked.

"Of course," Valodi responded. "I was with XCOM. Only for a short while, near the end, but we'd all heard of him."

"Lily is his daughter."

The leader's eyes widened. "And her father?"

"Still alive," Sam said. "But losing his daughter will be a terrible blow—maybe even a fatal one. But to be frank, she's a genius. I don't know that we can pull things off without her, even if he lives."

"You still won't tell me of the mission?"

Sam sighed. "I would rather not," he said. "Not here, in a settlement, where a thousand electronic ears might be listening. But you have the power in this situation. If I have to tell you to get your help, I will."

Valodi considered that. "When we first met, you said you were up to something big," he said. "I think maybe I've nevertheless been thinking too small."

"Game changer," Sam said.

Valodi nodded. "Okay," he said, "I can wait. Right now, we'll concentrate on freeing Shen. We can discuss the other matter when it's appropriate. What's the plan?"

Sam's relief was evident on his face.

"This is your city, so to speak," Sam said. "What would you suggest?"

* * *

Lena showed up while they were prepping the mission. She had a shotgun and was wearing a flak jacket, along with a highly determined expression.

"No," Amar said.

"I lost her," Lena said. "I'll get her back."

"You're not fully trained," he said.

"I'm trained enough," she said. "Put me out front, use me as a diversion. But let me come."

"Lena—"

"KB."

It stopped him cold. She had never called him that before.

"I heard the tone in your voice when I told you what happened," she said. "The doubt. There's some little part of you that thinks I might have turned her in. That I knew about my implant, and that this is all some elaborate plan. Can you tell me that thought didn't go through your head?"

He didn't want to hurt her, so much so that he was tempted to lie. But that wouldn't help anyone, least of all Lily Shen.

"No," he said, "I can't. Do I really believe you would betray us? No. But I have to consider the possibility. If I didn't, I wouldn't be doing my job. I wouldn't be faithful to the mission. When it comes to you, my judgment is suspect, because I'm so . . ."

He stopped himself there.

"So what?" she asked softly.

"You know," he murmured.

"I'm not sure I do," she said. "Maybe I don't know anything. But I need you to have faith in me. Please."

It hung there between them, and everything seemed to turn on that pause. But he knew what he had to do.

"Lena, you can't go," he said. "That's my final word."

He saw the hurt in her eyes, and he wanted to take her in his arms. But this wasn't the time for that. He had to focus.

He tried not to watch her walk away.

CHAPTER 14

AS MESSY, PERSONAL, and idiosyncratic as the settlements were, the New Cities were all the same. The ADVENT administration liked to claim that their carefully planned communities had sprung from the ashes of the old—that their foundations were New York, Mexico City, Mumbai, Beijing, but there were a couple of things wrong with this assertion. The first was that only a fraction of Earth's cities had been reduced to rubble in the conquest—most of the world's governments had capitulated after the first few were trashed. Instead, Earth's urban centers had been meticulously deconstructed and replaced after hostilities ceased. So in most cases, there had been no ashes to spring from.

The second fact of the New Cities was that they preserved nothing of the old within them. One could stand where Paris or München or New Orleans had once stood and not know the difference between one and the other. No Notre-Dame Cathedral, no Hofbräuhaus or

Jackson Square. ADVENT propaganda maintained that in this sameness was equality—that it dissipated the sort of national, regional, and ethnic pride that had once led to bigotry, war, and pogroms. This was another way of saying that the human race was being cut off from its history and what it had accomplished—good and bad—in the millennia of civilization before the aliens came. The cities were not built by humans, but for them, like the habitats in a zoo, but on a far grander scale.

During the day, New Kochi was a city of glass and steel, air and light. There was no mixture of architectural styles; instead, the same modular elements repeated themselves in different combinations and at varying scales. Green space and water features like fountains were evenly distributed throughout the city, but none of those fountains featured tritons or swans or little boys peeing. They were simply jets of water that went up and came down. There were statues, however, portraying humanlike aliens and alienlike humans while avoiding the nasty reality of, say, the Chryssalid that had killed Thomas. The most striking sculpture was that of a tall, lean alien with a bulbous head and huge eyes. It held hands with a reclining human, and it was supposed to look like the alien was helping the human back on his feet. Amar always thought it looked more like the alien was leaving a pleading human behind. In every New City Amar had ever entered, some variant of that statue could be found in the public squares.

The cars that wandered the wide street grids were as difficult to tell apart as the buildings, and they moved at highly controlled speeds. ADVENT claimed to have reduced traffic fatalities to nearly zero, which was probably true, since they didn't consider or even gather any statistics beyond the city limits.

Billboards like the ones in the settlements recounted the "news," but were much, much larger.

They made their way into New Kochi at night, using the remains of an old sewer system the resistance had tied into the shiny, highly efficient new one.

At night, New Kochi appeared more sinister. There was plenty of light, but light like one might find in a prison camp—high beams shone down from tall buildings, the dull red glow of scanners that citizens were required to submit to now and then. But the presence of troopers was slight, and they interacted with people in an almost friendly sort of way. It accounted for the very different ways in which Lena and Amar saw them, at least initially. Growing up, he had been afraid whenever ADVENT troopers came into Kuantan. They did rough searches, beat people, took them away. Lena had grown up thinking of them as protectors, and even felt relieved when she saw them. They indicated that she was safe from the dangerous dissidents.

That was another reason she shouldn't come along, he told himself. But the look on her face when he had last seen her haunted him.

They split into two groups immediately upon arrival. One was led by Abraham, one of Valodi's lieutenants. He had a motley squad of six, armored head-to-toe and bristling with weapons. Then there was Amar's group. They were dressed in New City street clothing purloined over the years by the local Natives. They each had a handgun concealed beneath light rain jackets. Dux and Amar had colorful duffel bags thrown over their shoulders, as if they were possibly off to play a cricket match.

Valodi had charted them a path to Processing that avoided scanners, and they didn't have much trouble staying clear of troopers. As they had hoped, they blended in on the crowded streets—no one gave them a second glance.

There were certain inevitabilities about how a police station was organized, but the ADVENT administration had neatly dissected the task of dealing with those who broke a law of some sort from that of "processing" anyone they thought might be a security threat. There were therefore no police desks where statements could be taken, or anything of the sort. Instead there was a series of holding and interrogation rooms around a central hub.

The building itself was round—a clean, modern structure of a single story surrounded by an immaculate lawn. The one thing that set it apart was its lack of windows. Instead it had glowing panels that suggested the interior was aquamarine, then pastel pink, then ecru, viridian, and so on.

"Okay," Amar said. "Now we just have to wait."

He watched the stream of humanity around him, wondering which ones had been born here and which lured in. Most of what he knew about their lives came from Lena, but it was still hard for him to imagine. He knew some of them worked for the ADVENT, and knew also that didn't make them evil any more than Lena was. Misguided and misinformed, perhaps, but not evil.

He desperately hoped they had the good sense to clear

when things started. The last thing he wanted was any sort of collateral damage.

The wait ended with a muffled explosion in the distance as Abraham and his group began their diversion—an attack on a gene therapy lab. Amar heard a few screams, and the people around them picked up their pace, moving away from the area until they were almost alone on the street—just what he had hoped for. Perfect.

"Let's go," Amar said.

They opened the duffel bags, where their weapons were waiting. Full armor was a luxury they could not afford for this mission.

"Dux," Amar said.

"Yep," he replied, settling the rocket launcher on his shoulder.

The few remaining people on the street cleared off, fast.

The rocket blew the door in, and they all quick-timed it across the street. Although humans worked for the ADVENT, intelligence suggested that they were never employed in processing centers. Amar prayed that was true. Of course there would be prisoners inside, but they should be well away from the blast. He knew all of this, but his breath drew cleaner when they came through the door to find only the ADVENT troops picking themselves up from the rubble.

One of them was a captain. Nishimura went at him with her sword. Amar and the rest turned their attention—and their weapons—to the others.

The surprise and the explosion turned out to be a huge advantage, and they shortly had the room cleared. Amar put Chitto at the front door to deal with reinforcements coming from outside. Then they began searching for Lily, one corridor at a time.

Most of the cells were empty, but a few were occupied, and they released the prisoners they found, who either fled without a word or babbled thanks before doing so.

They didn't encounter any resistance until they tried the third corridor, where they were greeted by magnetic rifle fire.

"No grenades or rockets," Amar said. "Shen may be in there."

He leaned in and took a shot. He missed, but he saw there was a pair of troopers on either side of a door that led into the next room. They were about six meters away.

They answered him with by shooting through the wall. If he'd been standing an inch nearer the door, he would have been hit.

"Okay," he said. "High-low. Nishimura, you stay low."

"Got it, Chief," she said.

Chief? It took him an moment to realize that she was talking to him. But Lena had called him that, too, hadn't she? In a joking way, yes, but . . .

"Go," he said.

He and Chakyar leaned around their respective walls and began firing at the troopers, head-high. Nishimura dropped to all fours and scrambled up the corridor.

When they stopped shooting, one of the jabbers stepped out to return fire. Nishimura cut his arm off. Then she dropped to the floor as the second trooper began shooting at her, stepping from cover as he did so.

Amar and Chakyar opened up again, riddling the armored figure with bullets.

Out in the central room, Chitto's rifle spoke out.

"Okay," she said. "Any time you guys are ready. Things are getting a little interesting out here."

Nishimura stood back up and took a quick look into the room. She jerked back, raising her weapon, but then stood strangely still.

"Nishimura?" Amar said. What was wrong with her?

She turned, and he saw. Her eyes were blank, dead-looking, and faintly phosphorescent. She raised her sword and charged.

Chakyar shrieked in terror and opened fire. Nishimura ignored the bullets and cut toward his head. He got his arm up, and his scream turned to one of pain as the sharp blade bit through his armor.

Amar dropped his weapon and grabbed Nishimura's blade arm, twisting it so that she dropped the weapon. He punched her in the chin and sent her sprawling.

"Dux!" he yelled. "Sit on her."

Then he picked up his assault rifle, took a deep breath, and ran down the hall. Before he reached the end of it, something was trying to get into his brain.

It started like pins and needles at the base of his skull, and then began quickly creeping around toward his face, like a foot falling asleep. His thoughts went soft and strange, like words in a foreign language he almost understood and, if he paid attention for a moment, probably would understand. . . .

He blinked. He'd missed some time. How much?

He was in the room. He saw someone he thought he recognized, and there was something else, tall and lean and gray, with huge eyes . . .

A Sectoid . . .

What was he supposed to be doing? He needed to know what to do.

And the voice began to tell him—was telling him—when something hard and cold rose up from deep inside of him, clotting behind his eyes, forming an image. A picture, a snapshot. Rider, lying on the ground, her lifeless eyes staring up at him. Her cold lips twitching.

"Shoot it, dumbass," she said.

It was like a rubber band snapping inside of his head. He pulled the trigger and felt the recoil of the weapon, saw green tracks walk up the alien's body, felt it pull out of his mind like a snail from a shell.

He vomited, and the colors behind his eyes faded to black and gray. The muscles of his ribs and chest knotted into spasms, and he fell to the floor.

Then someone was standing over him.

"You'll be okay," she said. "It will pass. I know."

It was Lily Shen.

"It was a Sectoid," she said. "Modified. Bigger and stronger."

She helped him stand.

* * *

Nishimura was propped against the wall, her hand over a hole in her armor, red leaking from between her fingers.

Her pupils were huge and her breathing ragged.

"Chief," she said. "Don't know what happened. Jesus. What happened? "

"Never mind that now," he said. "Don't worry about it. Let's just get you out of here."

"I think I can walk," she said.

"Just stay here," he said. "Keep pressure on your wound."

Chakyar had been cut to the bone, but fortunately Nishimura missed the joint of his arm, or else the whole thing would probably be off. Still, he'd bled enough to fill a bucket.

Amar moved up to where Chitto was taking aim.

"Four of 'em out there," she said. "Probably be a lot more, soon."

"Yeah," Amar said. "Dux, get those two on the right, then we'll run for it. Chitto, you cover our backs. I'll carry Nishimura."

He heaved her up over his shoulder and couched his weapon under his arm. Chakyar couldn't hold his rifle up, so he slung it and took out his pistol.

"Go!" Amar said.

Dux fired, and a car went up in a fireball, taking out the two jabbers hiding behind it. Then everybody ran but Chitto. Mag rounds screamed by him, tearing into the street, spattering against buildings. Then, he heard the bark of Chitto's rifle—once, twice, three times. He risked a quick look back and saw she was now following them.

After that it was all blurry, a nightmare dash through the city streets, civilians screaming, the whine of aerial patrols and floodlights searching through the night. He knew they were being followed when red streaks smacked into the building ahead of them, but there was nothing for it now but to try to stay ahead of them, reach the sewer, and get out.

They came around a corner and found themselves face-to-face with Abraham and his men.

"Keep going," Abraham said. "It's just down that way. We'll be along soon."

"Thanks," was all he could manage.

* * *

What seemed like an hour later, they emerged outside of the city, where Valodi and more of his men were waiting for them. Someone took Nishimura from him, and in a daze, he followed Valodi back to the settlement. Nishimura and Chakyar were carted off to the infirmary, or what passed for one.

Amar sat outside, breathing, trying to forget what had just happened, the thing in his head. He felt like a tunnel spider had walked into his mouth and built a nest there, like it was still in him and always would be. He had heard plenty from old-timers like Thomas about the aliens with psi-powers, but somehow he hadn't quite believed it and had thought that, even if it was true, only the weak-minded would succumb to such an intangible weapon.

If so, then he now knew he was weak-minded. If it hadn't been for Rider . . .

But Rider was dead. He didn't believe in ghosts. And

yet *something* had broken the contact, if only for an instant. Something had stepped up, if not from outside, then from within him.

"Hey," Valodi said. He'd been in a hushed conference with some of his men. "You look like you could use some of this." He proffered a bottle of clear liquid, which he knew from experience contained hooch fermented from palm sugar.

Amar did very much want a drink, but he feared it would make things worse, not better. He didn't want anything else messing with his brain.

"No thanks," he said. His mind was sluggishly starting to piece together the last awful moments of their flight from New Kochi. "Abraham. Did he make it back?"

Valodi shook his head. "I fear not," he said grimly.

"What about the others?"

Valodi squatted down and put a hand on his shoulder. "Their orders were to make certain you got back. That they did. I am proud of them."

Amar took that in. He wanted to cry, but he was too tired.

CHAPTER 15

WHEN VALODI WAS gone, Lily Shen joined him. She had never seemed very emotional, but now she had a sort of constant frown. He wanted to rail at her, tell her how stupid she'd been, how her actions had led to good people being killed. But she wasn't really stupid. She knew all of that already and didn't need him to sort it out for her.

"I'm so sorry," she said, her voice flat. "Lena tried to tell me—"

"Listen," he said wearily. "Forget all of that for now. What I need you to tell me is what they did. Did they implant a chip in you?"

"No," she said. "I don't think so. And Valodi's men tested me just now. Unless they've developed something new, no."

"Okay, good," he said. "Here's the main thing: Did you tell them anything? Is the mission compromised?"

Her face contorted a bit.

"You felt it," she said. "You had it in your head, too."

"That's exactly why I'm asking."

She put her head in her hands. "I told it everything," she whispered. "The mission, the Avenger, the Elpis, my father. I gave it all up. Everything."

Of course she had. How could she not?

"When?" he asked, as gently as he could.

She shook her head. "I don't know. It was in my head, and then there was gunfire, and you were there . . ."

He felt a faint glimmer of hope.

"So maybe we got there in time," he said. "Maybe we killed it before it could fill out a report or send a brain fax or whatever it is they do."

"Maybe," she said. "I hope so."

"Well," he said, "we'll find out, won't we? I'll send word to your father and Captain Laaksonen that we might be compromised. And hope."

She sat down and gathered her knees to her chest with her arms, rocking back and forth.

"Yes," she said. "Hope."

"Listen," he said, "it's been a rough couple of days. I can have you escorted back to the Elpis if you want."

She shook her head. "No. You'll need me to assess the target."

"If you're sure."

She nodded.

"If I've screwed this all up," she said, "I want to be there if it falls apart. To see the consequences of what I've done and deal with them."

He accepted that with a nod. He wondered where Lena

was and wished that she were with him. But he stopped short of trying to find her and went to bed instead.

Chances were very good that she didn't want to see him anyway.

* * *

Amar had been asleep for about two hours when one of Valodi's people—Miriam, he thought her name was—shook him awake.

"There's an ADVENT patrol coming," she said. "A big one. Valodi thinks they may be heading toward the infirmary."

Amar rubbed the sleep from his eyes and reached for his weapon; he'd fallen asleep in his armor.

The infirmary? It made sense. ADVENT had to know that some of them had escaped, despite the sacrifice of Abraham and his squad. It wouldn't be all that hard to figure out that some of them were injured; Nishimura and Chakyar had left plenty of blood in the processing center and probably a trail of it on the street. Any sort of medical facility in the settlement would naturally be the starting place for a search.

"Can you lead me there?" he asked Miriam.

"Yes," she said. "Quickly. The rest of your people are being gathered."

"Infirmary" was probably too fancy a word for the place, just a few beds and an operating table. Nishimura was still on the table, and a man in an off-white apron was fussing over her. Valodi was there, shouting orders to his men and women. Amar didn't see Chakyar anywhere.

"How is she?" he asked the doctor.

He shook his head. "She shouldn't be moved," he said.

Amar examined her. She had been stripped of her armor, and bandages were wrapped around her belly, where some blood was leaking through. Her face was still, but he could see that her eyeballs were darting about beneath her lids. He shuddered to think what she might be dreaming about.

"Gut shot," the doctor said. "She's lucky it was a bullet rather than a mag round, but the damage was pretty extensive. I think I sewed everything up, but I can't be sure. If there's even a nick in anything, she'll get peritonitis or worse."

"We don't have a choice," Amar said. "I won't let the jabbers have her. Have you got a stretcher?"

"There's the one she came on," he said.

The stretcher was bloody but serviceable. They loaded her on it, and Valodi ushered them out the back door. Amar could already hear the approaching troopers, prattling in their outlandish language.

Nishimura groaned as he and Dux carried her through the winding alleys of the settlement. Behind him he heard shouts of outrage and screams of pain, but thankfully the jabbers' magnetic rifles remained silent. That would probably change if they caught sight of Amar and his companions.

Valodi led them to an old canal where three small boats awaited them. Amar and Dux laid Nishimura flat in one of them, but with her stretched out in it, there was no way to use the oars. He motioned Dux into one of the other boats and then eased himself into the water, hoping it wasn't too deep.

It came up to his shoulders, so he took the mooring line and began to tow the small craft in the direction Valodi indicated. Everyone else piled into the other boats and began to row.

There was no current. The water was warm, often thick with weeds, and smelled distinctly of sewage. He didn't even try to imagine what might be living in it, instead just concentrating on putting one foot ahead of the other. Behind him, Nishimura cried out. Not loudly, but it wasn't a whisper, either. A few minutes passed, and he thought everything was fine.

Then she screamed.

The jabber must have already been following the canal, maybe having heard her first cry. Amar hadn't seen her, but he did now as she stepped through a beam of moonlight striking the bank. He froze, hoping against hope the trooper wouldn't see them in the darkness, wouldn't think to look down into the canal.

She almost didn't, but then Nishimura whimpered. The shadowy figure stopped and raised its gun. Amar let go the line and sloshed toward the berm. He didn't have a chance, but he wasn't just going to stand there and take it.

Then a second shadow appeared behind the jabber. He heard a sort of choking gasp before the ADVENT soldier toppled into the canal. Amar saw moonlight flash on steel. Then whoever it was blended back into the shadows.

It could almost have been Nishimura herself, but she was still in the boat, breathing hard.

A little after midnight they made it to the river, which proved too deep for him to walk in, so he had to go around to the back and push the boat by swimming. Dux joined him, and together they made enough of an outboard motor to keep up with those rowing.

After about another hour, Valodi led them to one of the *kettuvallam*, the big houseboats, where his men helped him and his people aboard, Nishimura included. The doctor from the settlement checked her vital signs.

"Hard to tell," he said.

* * *

Amar dozed again and woke to Nishimura screaming something in Spanish. He groped his way to where she lay and took her hand.

"Nishimura," he said, "it's okay."

She gripped him back with her calloused fingers and gasped.

"KB?" she said weakly. Her hair was free of her bandana and looked like an oil slick on the white pillow. The hollows of her eyes were dark.

"Yeah, Alejandra," he said. "It's me."

"*Mi bróder*," she gasped. "*Estamos in el infierno*?"

"I don't understand you," he said softly. "You're speaking Spanish."

"Are we in hell?" she asked.

"Not yet," he told her. "Although I don't blame you for thinking so."

She grunted.

"It feels like we're in hell," she said. "I thought I saw Toby. He was . . ." She stopped.

"Something happened," she wailed. "What happened?"

"You were shot," he said. "You've got a nice wound in your belly, so don't move around too much. You'll start it bleeding again."

"I don't remember," she murmured. "*Asu, no me acuerdo . . .*"

"It's okay," he said.

She fell silent, and he thought she had drifted off to sleep. But then she stirred again. "It's not true," she said. "I do remember. I just wish I didn't."

"It got in my brain, too," he said. "I understand how you feel. There was nothing you could do."

"Did I kill anyone? Chakyar . . ."

"No. Chakyar will have sore arms for a while, that's all."

"Did anyone get killed?"

"No. None of ours, anyway." He could tell her about Abraham and the others later.

She took a long breath and winced. "I'm in pretty bad shape, huh?"

"You'll live," he said.

"Yes," she said. "I'll live. So I can cut the throats of every last one of those sons of bitches."

The next day, he sent Nishimura to the Elpis for medical attention. There, she had a chance. Where they were going, she had little to none, despite her attitude.

* * *

The first leg of their trip was in the *kettuvallam*, following the course of the Muvattupuzha River north and east, then further along on the smaller flow of the Killiyar. The boat was a comfortable fourteen meters long, with bedrooms, toilets, and a small galley. Although the wood-and-wicker houseboats had once served as cargo vessels moving spices through the backwaters, in the last few decades before the invasion they had been redesigned as tourist craft, affording a quiet, comfortable exploration of the area. Now they had been repurposed once more into movable living space and smuggling vessels.

Like the Mississippi Delta where they'd found Lena, much of inland Kerala was returning to an untamed state. What had once been rice paddies were now full-on swamps, complete with mugger crocodiles sunning on muddy banks, pythons, hornbills, and a bewildering variety of plants and animals. It reminded Amar very much of the country of his birth.

Lena had been avoiding him since Lily's capture and rescue, and he was inclined to give her the space she wanted. Something had gone wrong in Piravom, and it was because both of them had lost focus—because they had been too busy making goo-goo eyes at one another. More rested upon his shoulders now, and he felt it, knew how close he had come to letting it all fall apart.

And she had asked him to have faith in her, and he had shown her that he didn't. She probably didn't know how much that had hurt him to do, and he wasn't going to tell her. If she didn't want to talk to him, it was better he leave it that way, at least for now, if not forever.

Their boat ride ended in what had once been a small village, but which now served as a hiding place for munitions, fuel, and two all-terrain vehicles. Valodi and two of his men debarked with them. The rest began their voyage back south.

They traveled dirt roads for several kilometers before reaching a narrow blacktop road in surprisingly good condition. From there the country got hillier and drier, but as their elevation increased, the vegetation grew lusher. They returned to dirt roads, and at times Valodi's man Mitchum had to clear the trail with his sword. Mitchum was a compact, dark-sinned American in his fifties, a bit on the brash side. It was he who had killed the jabber at the canal.

Amar felt safe under the rainforest canopy, safer than he'd felt in a long time, even on the Elpis. He knew it was an illusion but decided to take what little comfort he could get.

On the morning of the third day, as he went down to a nearby spring to wash his face, he saw a lithe form moving through the shadows. He stood very still, watching the tiger pass, with a sense of wonder and no small measure of terror. Even though he knew intellectually it wasn't likely to attack him, its very shape and the way it moved sent alarms through his primate brain, which had evolved largely to avoid tigers.

He suddenly felt a profound awareness of the world, a connection to it that all of the hiding and fighting and death had pushed deep into his marrow. In that moment, he remembered that the world was beautiful, and that he was a part of it, would always be a part of it. As Rider and Thomas and Toby were still a part of it.

He had grown up with a large menu of things to believe about the afterlife, and he had never subscribed to any of them, not specifically or with any conviction. But it was good to be reminded of the wonder of it all, the dread and ecstasy of existing.

The tiger turned and stopped, its eyes fixed on him, and for what seemed an eon they locked gazes. Then the great cat faded into the jungle. As it went, Amar felt as if the ghosts that he had been carrying were now following the great beast, and he didn't know whether he felt sadder or more relieved. But he felt he was a little bit lighter.

When he returned to camp, Chitto looked at him strangely.

"What?" he asked.

"You look different, Chief," she said.

He smiled.

"I saw a tiger," he told her.

* * *

The ship had flattened a swath of forest when it crashed, but the jungle was doing its best to take it in, as jungles tended to do. It was huge, so huge that at first he wasn't sure what he was looking at. It could have been an odd upthrust of stone. But when they were closer, and he could see beyond the climbing vines and dense young growth around it, it became obvious that it was nothing the natural world had produced.

From what little he knew about the aliens, he had been expecting something disc-shaped. He'd been wrong. It was somewhat boxy, longer than it was wide, thickest in the middle and tapering off at either end. Two winglike struts did support large saucer-shaped structures that were almost certainly its engines.

"It seems to be remarkably intact," Lily said, running her fingers along the metal of the hull. "The force of its crash must have been terrific, and yet there's hardly a scratch."

"Everything could be jelly inside," Sam said. "The fact that it's been here so long, undiscovered, speaks to the probability that the crew must not have survived."

"Yes," Mitchum said. "But they didn't all die in the ship. Look."

Amar hurried over to where he stood, near the perimeter of the crash site. The empty eyes of a skull looked up at him, but it wasn't human. It had a smallish hole in its forehead and a much larger one in the back.

"Looks like a Sectoid," Sam said. "The old kind."

Amar felt a tremor at the name, remembering the monster that had turned Nishimura against them.

They did a careful sweep around the area and found dismembered bones from both humans and aliens, but no intact bodies. Tigers and other beasts were probably responsible for that. But from their wounds, they all seemed to have been killed in a firefight.

"We're sure these guys were XCOM?" Amar asked.

"There are no records that a squad ever made it here," Sam said. "The location came from satellite data, not reconnaissance."

"People lived in this area back then," Valodi pointed out. "I believe there was a military outpost not terribly far from here. I can imagine it wasn't hard to miss this thing coming down."

"Secure a perimeter," Amar told his squad. "Doc, what next?"

"Well, we'll want to get inside," she said.

That didn't prove terribly difficult; whoever bones now lay scattered about the ship had left a hatch open in the back of the craft. Mitchum cleared back the vines and saplings, and then Amar peeked inside.

Something jumped. He had a brief impression of a figure that was somewhat humanoid, but which wasn't human—it was too small, its limbs were too long, it had a tiny head . . .

His finger eased off the trigger as the frightened macaque leapt from the interior of the craft and vanished into the trees.

Amar had seen any number of ADVENT transports and even the occasional gunship like the one they had encountered in the Atlantic. It was possible he'd seen some of their long-range craft in the distance. But this was something new to him.

ADVENT technology had been designed to set humans at their ease, to seem at least a little familiar, even if what lay under the hood wasn't recognizable at all. Here, that layer of familiarity wasn't present at all. He could stare at some of this stuff for years and never be able to guess what it was.

In other words, it was alien.

And dead. No lights flickered on consoles; no panels glowed with pale light. Aside from the cones cast by their torches, the ship was dark. And a tomb. Things had died here, too, and the tigers hadn't fooled with them. He didn't blame them. The whole place gave him the shivers.

Lily didn't say much, but she took a lot of notes. Amar stayed with her; the fact that the first thing to jump out at them had been harmless (well, close to it—macaques could give you a pretty nasty bite) didn't set him at all at ease. Not all of the aliens had been flesh and blood. He remembered they had robots and drones as well.

But after several hours, nothing had coming whirring to life to try and end him.

Lily didn't stop when the sun went down but instead worked long into the night. Amar split up the squad into thirds so they could watch her, keep watch outside, and get some rest.

He awoke the next morning with someone prodding his ribs. It was cool, and misty, and for a moment he was disoriented. Then he saw it was Lily.

"It's time to go get my father," she said.

Part III
The Avenger

"We have paid a heavy price,
but our efforts have not been in vain."

—DR. VAHLEN, XCOM CHIEF RESEARCH SCIENTIST

CHAPTER 16

AMAR WATCHED THE trucks arrive with more than a little trepidation. Valodi didn't like these guys, and Valodi dealt with some pretty horrifying people. He supposed they couldn't be picky, not at this stage of the game. Anyway, it was Sam's call.

They were several kilometers from the location of the alien ship, just off the main road in a field surrounded by forested hills. It had rained in the night, and the cool lingered, although by midday it would probably feel like a steam bath.

Amar didn't glance around to make sure everyone was in place. He didn't want to give anyone away.

The doors opened, and a rough-looking crew stepped out. The leader was a short, thick man wearing an old flak jacket that was too big for him and a helmet that wouldn't have looked out of place in World War II. He also had a knife the size of a cutlass and a submachine gun.

"So," he said, "we're here to talk."

"We appreciate you coming," Sam said. "And so promptly on time."

He was being sarcastic, although he didn't show it in his tone. They were four hours late.

The man shrugged. "We encountered ADVENT patrol."

"Where?" Amar asked.

"No worry, they did not see us," he replied.

He sounded pretty sure of himself, but that meant exactly nothing in Amar's book.

"Are you Kasparov?" Sam asked.

"Call me Caspar," he replied. "You know, Caspar?"

Sam looked at him blankly for a moment, then shrugged. "Caspar," he said. "I'm told you're good at getting things."

"Sure. What you want? Liquor? Chocolate? Woman, maybe?"

"No," Sam replied. "For starters, I need cuprate-perovskite ceramic. I need a cryogenic still, a variety of rare earths, diamond lasers . . . Well, here, why don't you just take the list."

Caspar took the paper and looked at it incredulously. "This is all very difficult," he said. "Dangerous things to get."

"Sure," Sam said. "And we'll pay you for that. And for your discretion."

"Some will have to be 'liberated' from ADVENT Administration."

"I'm aware of that also," Sam said. "The price will be fair."

Unless he was lying, Sam didn't know who their financial benefactors were any more than Amar did; only the Shens had that knowledge, and they were guarding it, at least for now. When Sam was being candid—which usually involved a glass or two of the stuff they were distilling from coconuts—he speculated that there was a network of donors, some of them possibly even inside of the collaborationist governments.

There were rumors that some of those who had sided with the aliens in the beginning only did so to be on the inside, to bide their time until the moment was ripe to take action. To Amar, this had always seemed like wishful thinking. Now he was starting to believe it was possible.

But all he really knew was that currency arrived, usually in the form of valuable trade goods.

"Let's see what you have to trade," Caspar said.

Sam motioned him behind their truck and threw open the flap.

"Antibiotics," he said. "Electronics. Whiskey—real whiskey; I have no idea where they got it, but it's good Scotch. Power rations. Have some hacks, too, for detecting implants, and also some counterfeit implants. You can really only use them once or twice, but you understand the possible benefits."

The latter were things the Shens were now producing themselves.

"So this is my upfront, then?" Caspar said.

"Oh, no, no, no," Sam told him. "This is just so you see we're bargaining in good faith."

"Well, that's very interesting," Caspar said. "But I think we'll take it up front."

"Well," Sam replied, "then I suppose we'll have to find another bunch of feckless hyenas to do business with. Too bad. This is going to be big, and you could have been part of it."

"Sure," Caspar said, lifting his hand and drawing it across his throat.

Then, he looked a little surprised. He repeated the motion.

"Oh," Amar said. "We took the precaution of disarming the snipers you sent in here yesterday. They're perfectly fine. And their positions have been filled with our own sharpshooters."

One of the men reached for his gun and then spat out a groan as a bullet smashed through his shoulder. A few seconds later, they heard the report.

"This is awkward," Sam said as the man swore and sank to his knees. "We were really hoping to avoid any bloodshed, and now look. Do you think you could help us keep things at this point, Caspar? Help end the violence?"

The man glared at him but nodded grudgingly.

"Here," Sam said. "Take the list. I have copies. If you're the first to bring me what I need, you'll get paid. And if you ever try to screw us again, we'll put the lot of you in the dirt. Is that good?"

"It's good," Caspar grated, after a moment. He and his men climbed back into their trucks and left.

"What if they turn us in?" Amar asked.

"That lot?" Sam said. "ADVENT would shoot them on sight. Caspar might die knowing he got his revenge, but I don't take him for that sort. For one thing, he hates the aliens. Us, he's merely put out by. He may even come around one day. We might be buddies."

"I don't know about that," Amar said, "but if he can get us the stuff, I'll put up with a lot."

* * *

Back at the ship, a village was growing. But it wasn't huge, and its inhabitants were a pretty select bunch. Captain Laaksonen—now entirely in charge of the Elpis—was quietly bringing on board scientists, engineers, machinists, and chemists from around the globe, where they were carefully moved by the Valodi's people along the route Amar and the rest had followed to the crash site.

A number of huts had been constructed, and solar panels provided most of their energy. The population was now thirty, enough to make Amar start to feel edgy. The more people, the more likely they were to be noticed by the ADVENT, especially when people and materials were moving into and out of what was supposed to be a restricted area.

He spent a lot of his time trying to fortify the area as well as he could. Components for a few larger guns found their way to him, which couldn't hurt—but what he was most interested in was early detection. He established lookouts up to two kilometers away and set up motion-activated cameras along every trail big enough for a bicycle.

A few days after their meeting with Caspar and his men, one of the lookouts broke radio silence, transmitting a short, encoded message:

Inbound transports. Five. Search spread.

Amar had been taking a much-needed rest in his

hammock when the message came. He rolled out and picked up his assault rifle.

"Incoming," he shouted. "You know your positions. Get to them. All non-coms—into the ship."

They had run this drill a few times, so it went relatively smoothly, despite the panic that overcame a few. Amar's own gut was tight.

In all of his earlier encounters with the ADVENT, there had been an objective, or they had been in the wrong place at the wrong time. In either case, after winning the fight, they were free to hightail it out of there.

But here the objective was to resurrect the Avenger, which was what Dr. Shen had begun calling the alien ship. At this point, the Avenger wasn't something they could carry with them. Whether the transports represented a random patrol—or worse, a targeted one, triggered by, say, Caspar turning them in—they were screwed. Even if they killed every trooper in all five transports, the ADVENT could just keep sending soldiers until they were overwhelmed.

If they were spotted now, it would be over before it had even really begun.

Moments later they heard the purr of alien engines. Amar searched what little he could see of the sky. He thought he saw a metallic flicker. Then it was gone.

He was just starting to breathe again when a shadow fell on him. He looked up through the trees and saw the aircraft moving over. Heart hammering, he checked his rifle for the third time.

The shadow continued on. Half an hour later, the lookouts gave the all-clear. It had been a routine patrol, and to all appearances, they hadn't been noticed.

It could be months before another such patrol came by. It could be hours. Either way, they were far, far from safe.

* * *

"We were wrong to assume the power was completely out," the elder Dr. Shen said, at the next day's briefing. Amar was invited to these meetings, although he often didn't understand much of what they were talking about. "There are certain key areas where there is a small amount of energy still manifesting itself, a kind of low-level maintenance, or perhaps even a long-term healing process."

"Are you saying the ship is alive?" Sam asked.

"Not in any biological sense," Lily picked up. "But the aliens' technology has a very complex set of feedback loops at every level, so you might compare it with, say, the human body. If a cell in your body is damaged, it either repairs itself or is replaced by neighboring cells. This happens without reference to the higher systems of the body, which govern health and healing at larger scales. If, for instance, you receive a bigger insult—a cut or gash—blood must clot, leucocytes must arrive to combat infection. Heart rate and blood pressure may adjust, and your cognitive system will modify behavior. On an entirely different level, intelligent beings will employ first aid—washing or disinfecting the wound, closing it up in some manner, and so forth. This ship is currently functioning, so to speak, mostly at a cellular level. The higher systems seem to be detached or at least in deep hibernation. For the most part, this is probably a good thing for us. Like their transports and other equipment, this ship was probably originally equipped with any number of safeguards against being taken over by anyone other than its creators. These are all shut down at the moment. We need to identify these systems and make sure that they remain dysfunctional when we turn the power back on."

The elder Dr. Shen tapped up a display of the ship they had mapped it thus far.

"Parts of the ship remain inaccessible to us," he added. "We don't even have a guess as to what they do. Some we have been able to open up using our own power sources. But this large section near the nose of the ship is a true enigma. It may be that only the computer can open this area, and there are a couple of problems there. The first is that we need power, and a lot of it. That is the next really crucial step in this project. It became clear to us in the early days of the war that the aliens had a power source far superior to anything we possessed. Other than a few confusing readings and a bit of research on fragments of their technology, we were never even certain what it was. Our research came to an untimely end.

"Of course the New Cities and everything the ADVENT Administration has built runs on this power source of theirs. In the twenty years since the conquest, Dr. Vahlen gathered a great deal of data concerning this matter, and as a result I can say that we now have a fairly firm grasp on it. The key is an element that does not seem to be naturally present on Earth—Elerium. When this ship crashed, it lost much of its Elerium. Indeed, it might have ejected it or neutralized it in some way. Of what remains, I have prioritized repurposing some of it for a more immediate use, since we don't have enough of it to bring the ship into a more responsive state."

"So we need more of this Elerium," Sam said.

"That is correct," Dr. Shen said.

"That shouldn't be a problem," Sam said. "It must be everywhere. All I need to do is alert our black market assets. Just give me the specs—how they can recognize it, how to handle it, all of that."

"Speaking of assets," Dr. Shen said, "There is another matter, one I do not believe we should involve the black market in—or, in fact, anyone outside the core of this group."

* * *

After so much time in open country, Amar had forgotten how confining the Elpis could be, especially for two people doing their best to avoid one another. And although he thought about approaching her every day, it was Lena who very typically broke their mutual silence first. He was in the Rathskeller at lunchtime, picking at his calamari when she walked in and saw that the seat across from him was the only empty one. She paused and turned as if to leave, but then, with her usual determination, proceeded to his table.

"Do you mind?" she asked.

"No, please," he replied.

Once she was seated, he nodded at her plate. "The cod?" he asked. "Really?"

"It's growing on me," she said. "We all have to adapt, right?"

"I guess so," he said.

"Good," she replied. She began eating. He tried to think of something to say, something to begin with, but he couldn't imagine where to start. So instead he just picked at his food.

"I saw Nishimura," Lena said. "Looks like she's doing well."

"Yeah," Amar said. "I ran her through her paces the other day. She'll be going along on this."

"Great," Lena replied. Then she returned her attention to the food. When she was done, she picked up her plate and looked as though she were about to leave. Instead, she turned back.

"It's a little crowded here," she said. "Could you meet me above when you're done?"

"Sure," he said.

* * *

Amar remembered talking to Lena by starlight and later—on the voyage from Gough Island to India—slow-dancing across the gently rolling deck, holding her in his arms. They were in those same seas now, but headed south.

Twenty years ago, they would have sailed east across the Arabian Sea to the Gulf of Aden and the Red Sea, through the Suez Canal and thence to the Mediterranean. But the aliens had trashed the canal, and so they had to go the long way, the way the Portuguese had in the fifteenth century, around the Cape of Good Hope.

The same seas, but a very different season, he thought.

She was waiting for him, arms crossed. He waited for her to say something.

"So," she began. "You and I, we're stuck together for a while. Not just on this ship, not just on this mission, but maybe for the rest of our lives, however long or short that may be. So let's adapt."

"I'm sorry," he said. "I know I hurt you . . ."

"You don't want to talk about that," she said. "To say I was hurt doesn't begin to cover it. Don't tell me you understand, because you don't. And that's not the point of this conversation."

"Is this where you say we should just be friends?" he asked.

She actually laughed at that. "We are not and have never been friends," she said. "I've been your captive; I've been the tagalong you were trying to get rid of; I've been your makeout buddy; and I've been the girl you've been avoiding like poison. But I have never been your friend."

"Wait," he said. "Back up one second. You were avoiding me, too."

"Yes," she said, "because you were a jackass. You owed me the apology you started in the Rathskeller immediately, not a month later. And you owed it to me to tell me how you felt. But that would the hard thing for you, wouldn't it? You're very good at what you do, Amar. Good at being a soldier. You're one of the bravest people I've ever known when it comes to that sort of thing. But you're one of the most cowardly people I've ever known when it comes to your personal relationships. You have all of these justifications for what you do and don't do, but what it all boils down to is that the easier thing for you to do is back away from anything like real investment. What you don't have can't be taken from you, right? For you, quitting is always easier than trying."

She stopped and took a step back.

"Wow," she said. "I promised myself I wasn't going to rant like that."

"Pretty good rant," he said.

"I don't know if it's occurred to you, KB, but I've been having a pretty awful time these past few months. My sister died, and I'm faced with the fact that pretty much everything I've ever believed was a lie. I'm not used to death and shooting and explosions or being lost in the ocean. Not really my thing, except that now it is, inevitably, unavoidably. This has all been very hard on me. Maybe I used you as a crutch, I don't know. So maybe I bear some of the responsibility for this state of whatever-it-is. That doesn't really matter now. We are going to adapt. We have to work together, so we have to be able to communicate, especially when we get to the site. Maybe we can be friends. Maybe we can't. But we can work together."

Amar felt like saying a number of things. Like how hard it had been to lose Rider and Thomas and Toby. How hard it would be to lose Lena. That she was probably right about him, and that he would like to learn to be braver.

Instead, he just nodded and said okay.

"You know I'm going this time, right?" she asked.

"Of course," he replied. Not as if he had a say in the matter this time. This whole project was Lily's. He was just in charge of the muscle.

CHAPTER 17

THEY BYPASSED GOUGH Island for fear that it was being watched because of the incident with the gunboat.

They refueled instead at St. Helena, another speck in the Atlantic that had once been the final prison of Napoleon Bonaparte. Unlike chilly Gough, St. Helena was mildly tropical, but it was every bit as rocky and isolated.

They stayed for a day, and then proceeded north, stopping once more at Madeira Island before going on to their final destination.

The Elpis surfaced along a barren strip of beach on the coast of Brittany. The sky was gray with a few blue lenses here and there, and the wind tousled the treetops almost playfully.

Chitto stood watch on top of the ship as Amar went with Nishimura and Dux to secure the beach, after which Lily and Lena came down, followed by Chitto.

Lily had two bags, one of which felt as if it were full of

lead. They took turns carrying it.

That night they saw the lights of New Nantes in the distance and the next morning a settlement. They avoided both and moved deep into a contagion zone.

It was chilly but not quite cold, and the leaves on the trees were gold and crimson and brown, something Amar had heard of but never seen before. He found it really quite beautiful and slightly depressing. He remembered Toby's meditation on sunrise and sunset people, and wondered if one could make a similar speculation about people who were conditioned by temperate, northern, or tropical climates. In France, one was faced with a yearlong cycle of death and rebirth, of graduated change. Around the equator, death and rebirth happened, too, of course, but not written on the landscape and installed on the calendar in the same fashion. Trees did not shed, appear to die, and then return to bloom. When something died in Malaysia, it was usually actually dead.

You could even say there were two seasons, wet and dry—but the psychological impact might be different.

He soon wearied of this. Toby had been overthinking things, and now so was he.

Sometimes they were able to follow a road, but more often it was easier to go cross-country. They passed overgrown petrol stations, an ancient abbey of crumbling gray stone, and a cemetery with hundreds of headstones. They cut their way through hedges and waded across creeks and slept beneath the stars—but more frequently under clouds.

One clear morning, under a rare cerulean sky, Amar called a halt because he wasn't quite sure what he was seeing. Across a field, something was moving at the forest's edge.

"What is it, Chitto?" he asked.

She raised her rifle to look, but after long moment, she didn't say anything. Instead she handed the weapon to him.

Peering through the scope, he saw what appeared to be a wild boar—no, three. One was closer and more obvious, but now he could make out the others a little deeper in. They looked as if they were confronting something; their legs were set and splayed, heads down, swaying from side to side in unison. The nearest looked very thin, almost emaciated, and most of its fur was gone, replaced by something that glinted in the sunlight, like glass or crystals.

"What am I seeing?" he wondered aloud.

"It's like they're guarding something," Nishimura said. "Or watching out for something."

"I'd like to have a closer look," Lily said.

"Not until I do," Amar said. "The rest of you stay here."

"Chief," Nishimura said. "You don't always need to be the one stirring up the hornets. Let me have a look."

He knew she was probably right, and certainly she was better suited for the job. But it was hard, putting someone else in harm's way. Easier on his conscience to go himself . . .

Lena didn't say anything, but he remembered her little diatribe about easy and hard.

So he did the harder thing and sent Nishimura.

He watched her move stealthily through the tall grass.

"Chitto, put that thing in your sights. The one in front."

He took out his field glasses and watched.

Nishimura stopped about ten meters from the animals, which did not appear to see her. Their eyes looked glassy and dead, but they were nonetheless swaying, occasionally stamping their hooves.

She took another few steps, and the nearest one charged her. He noticed its gait was odd, as if it were running on three legs.

Nishimura bounced back, bringing her weapon up. Then she abruptly fell backward, vanishing in the grass.

"*Asu!*" he heard her yelp. "*Miercoles!*"

Chitto shot it. The boar exploded like a puffball mushroom, except that instead of a cloud of brown spores, the pig seemed to sublimate into a sparkling, rainbow cloud.

"Oh, man," he said. "Nishimura, get out of there."

"It's okay, Chief," she said. "I just tripped."

He suddenly smelled something very strange, something he had smelled only once before, the night when they had seen the ADVENT soldiers using flamethrowers.

"Get back here, *now!*" he shouted.

He saw her reappear and start running.

"Contagion, do you think?" Lily asked.

After all of their trekking in so-called contagion zones, Amar had seriously begun to doubt the existence of any real contagion. It seemed more likely that ADVENT just wanted people roped off into areas where they were more easily controlled, and that the "contagion" was just another fabrication, a tactic to suck more people into the New Cities. He figured the guys they had seen that night were probably burning a pile of corpses or something, covering up their crimes.

It wasn't the first time he'd been wrong.

"Yeah," he said, "I think."

The other animals hadn't moved, but now one did, limping up to stand where the one that Chitto had shot had been.

"We should try to get a sample," Lily said.

"With all due respect, I don't think that's a good idea," Amar replied. "We've no idea how contagious it is. For all we know, we're already infected. But if we're not, I want to keep it that way. This mission has to come first."

"But if what we're seeing is really the contagion—it's the one thing we know the invaders really fear. It could be an important weapon to use against them."

"I will grant you that," Amar said, "but still believe we should try to get very far from here as fast as possible."

"I am in charge of this mission," she reminded him.

"Sure," he said. "Of *this* mission, not that one. Let someone else come study this some other time. Someone with the equipment to do so. We have nothing. No test tubes or petri dishes or whatever you need—we don't have it."

Lily sighed and looked at the remaining animals with what he could only describe as longing.

"Very well," she said.

* * *

Lily walked up beside him later that day.

"Thank you," she said.

"For what?" Amar asked, equally startled and confused.

"You were right," she said. "I am . . . impatient. I don't like to have time on my hands. When I see a problem or a puzzle, I want to solve it, right then, and I don't always think through what the costs might be. My father says I'm like a rabbit, always dashing ahead. In New Kochi I dashed ahead, and people died. So, thank you for asking me to take a step back."

Amar nodded. "You're welcome."

"You will probably be forced to do so again," she admitted.

"I know."

She laughed and swept her arm at the countryside. "How are you enjoying France?" she asked.

"I was expecting cheese," he replied. "So far, no cheese."

* * *

Two more days brought them to their destination, an old airfield deep in the countryside. The strip was cracked and grown up around the edges, but the control tower still stood, along with several large hangars. From the tower, Amar could see the ruins of a city and the river they had been paralleling for most of the trip.

They hadn't seen any more signs of the contagion— if that was in fact what they had seen—but Amar urged vigilance. He checked his own skin every few hours at first, looking for anything that was remotely sparkly, but now he was down to once a day.

In the overgrown hangar, they found what they had

come for—a thick, stubby, powerful-looking aircraft. It had wings, but they were short, and from the look of it, the craft relied more on jet or rocket propulsion for its motivation.

"I almost don't believe it," Lily said. "After all of these years. Once again, luck is with us."

"Some luck," Amar said. "A squad from Le Mans confirmed it was here last year, and the word got back to Vahlen."

"Is that a Skyranger?" Nishimura asked, a bit of awe in her voice.

"You've seen one before?" Lily asked.

"My father carved a wooden one for me when I was a little girl," Nishimura said. "He worked on it, you know."

"I didn't," Lily said.

"On the design, anyway," she said. "He was the propulsion engineer." She cocked her head. "It looks a little different than my toy."

"Bigger, probably," Chitto commented.

Lily ignored Chitto's quiet sarcasm. "The original Skyranger was shot down during the war," she said. "This one was a prototype for the next model. Several were being built at different locations, but this is the only one we know survived. It was never finished. It has never been flown."

"What use is it then?" Dux asked. "Spare parts?"

"No," Lily said. "We're going to finish it."

Amar walked around the flier, admiring it.

"It can land and take off vertically," Lily went on, "and in quite tight circumstances. And it will fit very nicely into the Avenger. The Avenger will serve as a mobile base, much as the Elpis does now. But we can't very well fly something that size into a New City to extract a squad. We need something smaller."

"No more walking," Chitto said. "Or pickup trucks."

"Exactly," Lily said. "As handy as the Elpis has been for keeping the resistance going, it's very slow. Our response time to global events is tallied in days, weeks, months, as you all know. We can now cut that down to hours." She was almost twitching with anticipation. "Now if you don't mind," she said, "I'm eager to get busy working on this thing."

After setting up a perimeter and watch schedule, Amar began inspecting what was left of the airbase in hopes of finding something useful—weapons, food, and so forth—but it appeared the place had been looted long ago, probably by the same resistance fighters who had informed Vahlen about the Skyranger. After that, he organized forays into the empty suburbs of the nearby town, which didn't turn up much either but did a little to ease the boredom. Lena and Lily were doing most of the work on the ship, which left the soldiers very little to do.

A week passed, and heavy clouds brought cold rain and mist. By then they had set up a barracks in the building beneath the tower and managed to get an old radio working, so they had a little entertainment and news from the outside world. Most of the music was from before the invasion, but there was also radio theater, which mostly adapted movies and books from the old days, but lately new, original content was coming into favor.

And most of what went out over the radio waves was more than it appeared to be. To get the news, you had to know what you were listening for. Anything important was couched in apparent nonsense, but if you knew the code it was decipherable. When the announcer said, for instance, that he would like to dedicate the next song to his dear old mother in New Paris—and then the song itself mentioned Marseille—it meant that it was time for the resistance cell near Marseille to carry out whatever they had been planning. "Sister" on the other hand, currently referred to a settlement, so "To my ailing sister in Berlin" was a warning that New Berlin ADVENT was making a big push in the surrounding settlements—or a specific one, again indicated by something in the song.

It was not a good system for conveying detailed information—that tended to happen in Morse code—but it helped to minimize radio traffic that the jabbers might be able to track. The broadcast network had been growing somewhat organically over the last decade or so, or at least so it was generally said. However, Amar was beginning to wonder if there wasn't a more centralized, guiding hand behind that, just as the Elpis and Wunderland must have been receiving their funding from someone or some group of people.

He was half-listening to the radio when Nishimura came in, wearing a rain poncho.

"Chief," she said, "there's something you need to see."

* * *

There were four of them: two boars, a dog, and a deer in a little cluster on the other side of the river. Under the overcast sky, they looked like they were covered in gray patches, but he was sure that if the sun had been out they would be scintillating like the ones they had come across earlier. Like those animals, these weren't doing much, just sort of bobbing, facing in their direction.

Amar felt cold in the pit of his belly.

"Do you think they followed us?" he asked.

"Maybe," Nishimura said. "Looks like they came from that direction, anyway."

"How can you say?" he asked. "They don't seem to move."

"Well, they weren't here yesterday," she said. "Maybe they only move at night. Or early in the morning. Or midday. But unless they grew there, they came from someplace else."

"For all we know, they did grow there," Amar said. "Or maybe it's something in the soil. Step on it and you become infected or whatever."

"Should I shoot them?" she asked.

"No," he said. "Set up a tree stand back there and watch them. I want to know what they do."

The next morning the animals were all still right where they had been—except for one of the dogs, which now stood on their side of the river. In addition, a hedgehog and another dog had joined the balance on the farther side.

A hedgehog, he thought. How could something be so ridiculous and so horrifying at the same time?

Amar hurried back to base to find Lily Shen. He found her hard at work, digging around in the engine panels. They had brought a few tools with them, but fortunately the base had a machine shop that was still pretty well stocked with tools, so she had everything she needed—except maybe time.

"How much longer before it's ready?" he asked.

"It's coming along," she replied. "Why, are we in a hurry? You think we've been spotted?"

"Not by ADVENT," he said. He explained about the animals while she continued tinkering.

"That's pretty curious," she said.

"I find *terrifying* a more apt word," he replied.

She shrugged. "Figure out what to do about it," she said. "That's your job. I'm busy doing mine."

After their conversation on the road, he was a little taken aback by her tone. But she was deep in this now, all of her resources focused on what she was doing. When she got like that, she didn't take the time to be considerate or kind. That required mental energy she didn't have to spare.

"You told me that you saw ADVENT burning something in the contagion zone back home," Lena said. "They probably know more about it than you do."

She made a good point. The one thing the old base had plenty of was fuel, stored in tanks underground. He wasn't sure he could build a flamethrower that wouldn't explode in his hands, and after a round table with the other soldiers, they decided it was probably better to make something like Molotov cocktails using detonators and cans filled with fuel.

By the time they had a few of them rigged, three of the animals were on their side of the river.

Dux pitched one of the cans. It hit the ground, bounced, and wobbled to a stop about a meter from the middle dog.

"Nice throw," Amar said.

"Bocce champion of Rosedale, Ohio, two years in a row," he said, grinning, running his thick fingers through his copper hair.

The animals didn't react to the presence of the can at all. Dux tossed another one, which almost bumped the first one. He took out the remote.

"Let's see about this," he said.

The can detonated very satisfactorily, spraying burning fuel in all directions. Amar flinched involuntarily and took a step back, remembering the immolation of Vahlen's island.

The animals continued to stand there, burning, until they collapsed into fuming piles. He didn't see anything sparkly in the air.

"Well," Dux said, "that works."

"I guess," Amar said. "What about the ones across the river?"

"I dunno. Maybe we could build a catapult or something. I could use a rocket, but I hate to waste ordnance on something like this."

"No," Amar agreed. "We're a long way from an armory."

"Hey, Chief," Chitto said, peering through her scope.

"Yes?"

"That stuff that's on the animals? The crystals or whatever? It's on a few of the trees, too. See? On the leaves?"

Now that he was looking, he realized he didn't need the rifle; he could see the shimmer when the wind blew.

He glanced down at the ground around his feet, where dandelions were beginning to put out their seed heads. If the contagion could get into plants, could it hitchhike on their seeds? Or their pollen? Because if so, in a few days it would be everywhere.

He watched the flames subside on the corpses. He hadn't worried much about a little smoke being noticed; they hadn't seen aircraft of any sort flyingover since their arrival. But if he had to set *everything* on fire? That would bring the ADVENT, fast.

"Build your catapult," he told Dux. "But don't burn anything else unless you have to."

But they had to. The animals kept crossing the river, and they kept burning them. On the other side, the infection seemed to be spreading. It was like everything had a light layer of frost on it, and more and more animals joined the party.

And here, as well as across the river, the dandelions were starting to open. He found some old filter masks in the machine shop and insisted everyone wear them. He doubted it would do any good, but it seemed better than nothing.

* * *

Two days later, at the two-week mark of their arrival at the airfield, Lily decided to put the Skyranger through a few tests. Amar felt unexpectedly excited when the running lights blinked on and the wheels on the landing gear began to turn. He found himself smiling broadly as the craft rolled out of the hangar. Like the elder Dr. Shen and Dr. Vahlen, it was a blast from the past, a reminder that humans had once been resourceful creators and inventors.

And a promise that they could be again.

Lena and Lily hadn't just "fixed" the Skyranger—they had altered the design. The craft had two engines in the back—like a jet—but the wings were really just struts now, supporting two massive engines that could rotate. He watched as Lily tested the hydraulics, pointing the engines down—the position they would be in for touching down or taking off vertically—and back, where they would augment the rear jets once they were in full flight. A fifth under jet beneath the craft completed the Skyranger's propulsion system.

"There's only so much I can do here," Lily said. "I have other modifications in mind once we get back to the Avenger. Let's fuel her up and run a few more diagnostics. Then I'll take her up for a test flight."

"That's it, then?" Nishimura asked. "We just get in and fly back?"

"No," Lily said. "We have one stop on the way."

"*Miércoles*," Nishimura grunted. "I've heard that before."

"I'll tell you about it while we're fueling," Lily said.

Amar had been present when the trip was planned, so none of what Lily said was a surprise to him or Lena, but the others, it had been determined, hadn't needed to know. If Amar and Lily were both killed, captured, or badly wounded, the whole thing was to be scratched anyway. But now it was time for everyone to know the next step.

"We've figured out why we can't turn the power back on in the Avenger," Lily said. "The heart of the whole system is the computer. If we go back to the organic analogy, it's the central nervous system, limbic system, and circulatory system all in one. While it's not put together like one of our computers—in fact, we're not sure how some of the pieces work—we have been able to parse out some of the functions. In doing so, we discovered severe damage to what for reasons of simplicity I'll call its central processor, even though in some ways it's more of an adapter. The memory and programs are all still there, intact, but there's nothing to coordinate them. We have no hope of learning to build one of these things anytime soon. So we're going to steal one."

"Where?"

"New Singapore, probably," Lily said.

"One little stop," Nishimura said, "halfway around the world."

By that time, the Skyranger was fueled. Lily and Lena began working through another checklist as Amar trudged down to the river with Dux to see what the latest in their contagion situation was. He was only about halfway there when Nishimura called him from the tower.

"Incoming," she said. "Two ADVENT transports bearing in from the northeast. From Paris, probably."

Perfect. Bloody hell.

"Get everyone to the hangar and in position," he shouted. "We may be taking that test flight all together."

"Chief, you better watch it," Nishimura advised. "One of them is circling around your way."

Even better. They might have satellite intel. It was possible the ADVENT had been watching them for days.

Amar saw the shadow overhead and realized the

transport had already arrived and was landing between Dux and him and the base. He motioned to Dux to move off to the west. The vegetation was thicker there and the terrain rougher, which would slow them down considerably, but at least they would be in cover. Behind him, he heard the jabbers debarking. He slowed and got behind a big tree, determined that he wasn't going to die from being shot in the back. Maybe the troopers still didn't know about the Skyranger—after all, it had been in the hangar until a few hours ago. He and Dux might be able to divert them here long enough for the others to escape with the ship.

Then he saw the other transport. It had settled beyond the river, which seemed like sort of an odd move. But he didn't have much time to think about it—the patrol was only a few meters from them.

He turned back to look toward the trail, searching for a target but knowing he wouldn't find one until they came in after him. He could see movement through the autumn leaves, but nothing substantial.

He heard a sort of low whooshing sound, and suddenly a dragon's breath billowed into the trees, setting them instantly ablaze. With sudden horror, Amar realized that they didn't intend to fight him at all; they were going to burn him out.

He backed away from the flames as more of the liquid fire sprayed through the undergrowth. It was completely unreal, and he felt like he was missing something. He had never seen jabbers carry flamethrowers before. Only that once, back in the Delta . . .

Oh, he thought. Of course.

He broke radio silence.

"No one shoot," he said. "They're not here for us. Stay hidden."

The troopers weren't out to get him, but the fire seemed to harbor a real grudge of some kind. The wind gusted up, pushing the flame downwind, toward them, and actually encircling them in the north, which was exactly where they needed to go in order to return to the Skyranger. If they weren't fast enough to get around it, the fire would push them into the river, which would mean they couldn't help but be seen by the troopers.

Why couldn't it be raining today? Amar wondered. But, of course, ADVENT wouldn't be here with flamethrowers if it were raining. Panting, he forced himself to reach a greater speed, willow branches whipping him in the face and the muddy ground sucking at his boots. The red wall in the north continued to lengthen, and flames behind them were catching up.

"We've got no choice," Dux said. "It's outstripped us. We have to go to the river."

Grimly, Amar agreed.

By the time they got to the water, Amar was so dizzy from all the smoke that he blacked out momentarily, coming to a minute later with Dux dragging him along the river's edge. The water was colder than seemed possible, and in moments his feet and legs were numb. He looked back upstream but all he saw was fire and smoke, so the worry that the jabbers would see them lessened.

How had they known that the contagion was here? Did they have some way of detecting it remotely? Or was there just a lot of it in this area, and they were following the leading edge to keep it in check?

They came to a tributary creek that was for the moment acting as a firebreak. It allowed them to get out of the water and start pushing back northward, where they would hopefully find the road and make their way back to the base. He was fairly sure they would be able to see the base from the next high hill.

He was right. The hilltop had an old, industrial-looking structure on it, made of brick with a flat tile roof that was dangerously dilapidated. With the aid of the sapling at the base of it, they were able to climb atop the aging structure and get a commanding view of the landscape.

The fire had consumed a huge swath of forest on the other side of the river, and he could see smoke boiling up from much farther to the southeast. He didn't see any ADVENT transports, which seemed like good news until he spotted the control tower of the airfield, burning like a torch.

The whole place had been overrun.

"Chitto?" he sent over the radio. "Nishimura? Anybody?"

His only reply was static. His heart sank.

"Let's go see," he told Dux wearily.

They hiked down to the road and were starting up it when his earphone crackled. He wasn't sure whether it was words or just a burst of static.

"Come again?" he said.

"*Chief . . .*" someone said, but then static swallowed the rest.

"You hear that?" Dux said.

Amar did, and he knew the big man wasn't talking about the radio. Over the low grumble of the flames rose a profound roar. He saw the transport dropping toward them and crouched, feeling like a mouse under a sky full of hawks.

But then he saw it wasn't a transport. It was the Skyranger, her jets blazing.

Nishimura was leaning out of the open hatch.

"Come on, Chief," she shouted. "Let's get the hell out of here."

CHAPTER 18

"**WELCOME TO NEW** Singapore," the young man said. He was pleasant-faced, with a wide smile and dark brown eyes. "My name is Jonathan," he went on as his fingers flickered over the glowing icons on the board in front of him. "I think you'll like it a lot here. New Singapore is the very best of the New Cities, lah? You're from which settlement?"

"Kuantan," Amar said. It felt funny to say because it was the truth—a single lonely truth in this place built of lies—and in contrast to everything else he was telling Jonathan. About why they had come here, how they wanted to finally feel safe and be part of something bigger than themselves, and on and on.

"Okay," Jonathan said, tapping his screen. "Great. You have some excellent choices when it comes to housing." He looked them over. "Not to be presumptuous," he said, "but may I assume you two are a couple?"

Amar glanced at Lena. "Yes," he said, taking her hand. Another lie.

"Wonderful," Jonathan gushed. "Do you have a preference of which district you live in?"

Lena studied the prospects. "What about this one?" she asked, pointing to one.

"Well, that's fine," Jonathan said. "Not as nice as some others, though. You can't just take the apartment itself into account; you have to consider what's in the neighborhood. And see, this one has a terrace." His voice grew more confidential. "If you're planning to start a family, I can get you something even nicer. Here in New Singapore, we encourage family life—the bigger the better. There are lots of perks for young parents."

"That's kind of private—"Amar began, but Lena cut him off.

"This other one has a balcony," Lena said. "That's the one I want. Don't you agree, dear?"

"Whatever you say, sun bear," he said.

"As you wish," Jonathan said, his tone making it clear that he thought they were making a mistake. "Now, will either of you be signing up for gene therapy today?"

"Not today, no," Amar replied. "This is all really new to me. I need a little time to adjust."

"I know it must be overwhelming, coming from a settlement," Jonathan said. "You can change your mind at any time, however—just visit your nearest therapy center. You may think you're perfectly healthy, but you might be surprised. The settlements are just repositories of filth, and—well, I guess you know, don't you?"

"Yes," Amar said. "Farewell, filth. Good riddance."

"Now, let's see about setting you up with a meal plan," Jonathan continued. "Nobody goes hungry in New Singapore!"

He ticked off a few things and then handed them each a small slip of plastic.

"Are either of you planning to work right away?"

"Actually," Lena said, "I was told there might be a job in Cybernetics Eight. An old friend of mine works there and has recommended me. I have an interview tomorrow."

"Well," Jonathan said, taking back her plastic. "Let me put a work visa on that, then. Sir, what about you?"

"I've got nothing lined up," Amar said. "But I would like a visa, if possible."

"Of course," Jonathan said. He finished up Lena's card. "Cybernetics, eh? But with a face like that, you really ought to be in hospitality. It's where all the real fun is."

"I'll bear that in mind," Lena said. "If the other thing doesn't work out."

* * *

"Why the high-rise and not the terrace?" Amar asked, as he examined their apartment on the eighty-fifth floor. Jonathan had called it small, but it was the biggest—and certainly the cleanest—place Amar had ever lived.

And it gave him the absolute willies. It was like being in the belly of a monster.

"Well, we want our privacy, don't we, dear?" Lena said. "If you live down in the community developments, everyone wants to be friends, and have you over for drinks, and hang out at the community pools and tennis courts and so on. The people in high-rises, not so much. They keep to themselves. A lot of them are shut-ins."

Amar, nodding, acknowledging that was something he wouldn't have known. He didn't like Lena being involved in this, but she was the only one who knew much of anything about living in a New City.

"Did you grow up in a high-rise?" he asked.

"Nope," she said. "I was a terrace girl, all the way. That's why I know we shouldn't be down there. It will be distracting, and well . . . you know."

The apartment had quiet pastel blue walls with recessed lighting that somehow did not cast shadows. It had three rooms—a general purpose area that contained a media screen, a couch, a small kitchen with a fridge, one burner, a microwave, and a few drawers that functioned as a pantry. The utensils and dinnerware were made of some lightweight filament that was disposable and recyclable. A balcony opened on one side, with room enough for two people to sit comfortably, and it looked out over the tidy city of New Singapore. The view was mostly of other high-rises, but a few slivers of ocean were visible in the distance.

The balance of the apartment included a bathroom with a shower, and a bedroom.

"One bed," Amar said.

"Well, honey," Lena said, "we *are* a couple. Otherwise we would be living in different places, right?"

He smiled and nodded, a little irritated at himself. This had all been talked about in the planning stages. No one knew to what extent New City residents were surveilled—whether or not the walls had eyes, so to speak. Sam hypothesized that apartments were probably wired, but that not every apartment was watched—with so many millions of people, that would be a staggering task. Instead, there were probably algorithms running, searching for particular turns of phrase and behaviors that would attract heavier scrutiny. So they had to be careful what they said, and to some extent what they did, but how careful? If he built an explosive device, it would likely be noticed. But would it attract attention if he slept on the couch? It was going to be hard, always imagining an audience that could be watching but never being sure what those watchers would consider suspicious. Since they were new arrivals, would surveillance be more heavily weighted toward them?

Or maybe no one was watching them at all. Most New City citizens had implants, which certainly monitored their behavior. Wiring apartments would be costly and redundant.

But why take the chance? They knew what they were supposed to do. They didn't have to talk about it, at least not much.

Lena cooked dinner for them, which consisted of a lump of CORE in a reddish sauce, green beans that were almost a meter long before she cut them down to size, and brown rice.

"The beans are really good," he said.

"Thanks," she replied.

"Really big."

She nodded. "I hear they're using this new fertilizer that makes vegetables grow to a humongous size. It's also supposed to make them more nutritious." She smiled in a slightly devilish fashion. "You should try the CORE. It's good with this sauce."

He stared at the vaguely ivory-colored stuff. Maybe he could pretend it was tofu. But just the thought of it almost made him gag.

"I'm really stuffed," he told her.

"I thought so," she said. "It's a good thing I'm not the sort to make fun of somebody for what they will and won't eat."

He took the jab. He deserved it.

He decided to risk sleeping on the couch. He was already too distracted by Lena's presence. Lying next to her would only worsen matters.

She watched him arrange his pillow. "We can switch tomorrow night, if you want," she told him.

"It's okay," he said. "Have a good night."

"You too," she said, closing the door.

He lay awake in the too-clean apartment, staring at the ceiling, feeling very alone and stupid.

We're going to adapt, she'd said.

And she had.

* * *

The next morning, they had coffee and sweet pastries, both rare luxuries outside of the cities. Lena smiled at his reaction.

"I wondered why you were all making such a big deal about that coffee Captain Simmons gave you," she said. "Now I get it. Coffee, tea, chocolate, all the stuff I took for granted growing up . . ." Her face lit up with excitement. "We should get drinks tonight. That horrible stuff you guys drink, and the way you feel the next day—*ugh*. They have the good stuff here. You're not going to believe how good it is. And ice cream. Have you ever even *had* ice cream?"

Amar didn't know if the room was wired, but his own algorithm gave him a sort of mental twitch when she said "you guys." He'd thought she had moved firmly into the XCOM camp, but maybe being back in a city—surrounded by the stuff of her old life, a life that comprised all but a few months of her existence—was making her think twice. She was certainly excited about being here. She wasn't acting.

"Drinks," he said. "That sounds good."

"Okay. So. I have my 'interview' this morning, and hopefully by the end of the day, we'll have something to celebrate." She finished up her coffee and roll. "Probably best if you stay here," she said. "It would seem strange to have a tagalong at the interview."

"That suits me," he said.

When she left, he dithered for just a moment, knowing that there was really no right way to deal with the situation. He was ashamed of his suspicions, but at the same time, at this point in the game, could he really allow himself to be blinded by his feelings?

He left the apartment and followed her.

* * *

He knew almost instantly something was wrong. They had both memorized the city plan. They had chosen

New Singapore because it was one of the few places that manufactured the component they needed. The plant was located at the edge of town. Lena was headed toward the City Center.

Maybe she was just trying to kill a little time sightseeing. The interview was at no particular hour—the objective was just to get her name in, to announce "I'm here" to their contact on the inside. The contact would then arrange for her to get clearance to enter the factory. When she'd said they would have cause to celebrate, she didn't mean because she would have a job, but because the next hurdle of their mission was cleared.

It didn't have to happen right away. But the quicker, the better, right? So it made sense for her to go in the morning. But she wasn't going there, and she wasn't wandering either. She knew where she was headed, and a few minutes later so did he, when she allowed herself to be scanned by an ADVENT trooper before entering a gene therapy clinic.

* * *

Amar returned to the apartment, trying to sort things out, but he was never able to come to a good conclusion.

He watched propaganda and a supposedly unscripted show about living in the settlements. It was meant to be funny, and if you had never lived in one, it probably was. He turned the media screen off. He took a shower. He waited.

Lena walked in toward the end of the day. She gave him a smile that seemed obviously false.

"I got the job!" she said. "I start tomorrow. Now, how about those drinks?"

His own smile probably seemed no more sincere than hers, but he tried anyway.

* * *

Like everything else in the city, the bar was clean and orderly, a far cry from some of the filthy ratholes he had frequented in his time. And Lena was right—the drinks were very, very good. Amar had drunk things called "whiskey," "vodka," and "tequila," but they had all pretty much tasted the same, like jet fuel. Here they were subtle, distinct, and didn't hurt his throat and sinuses on the way down.

"Well?" Lena asked. She had changed into a crinkled yellow sleeveless dress and looked like a flower planted in the place it was supposed to grow. He realized he enjoyed seeing her like this, which made him feel a little sick. He nursed his drinks carefully, trying not to get drunk. Because if he got drunk and started talking . . .

"You like it here, don't you?" he said.

Crap, he realized. Too late. The drinks were a lot stronger than they tasted.

"You mean this bar?" Lena asked. She wasn't exactly sober either and had in fact been drinking with more abandon than he had ever seen her do. Now that he understood how bad the outland hooch was, he sort of understood. Or maybe it was just because she felt comfortable here.

"The bar is nice," he said. "But that's not what I meant."

She pointed the index finger of the hand she was holding

her martini with. "You mean New Singapore," she said. It sounded like an accusation, albeit a lighthearted one.

"Right," he replied.

She leaned back and crossed her legs. The dress was short, and he realized he was seeing her knees for the first time. She gazed at him with an unreadable expression.

"Sure," she admitted. "It's familiar. It's not infested by bugs, snakes, or lizards. And this tastes good." She finished her drink and set it down for the bartender to replace. "I like air conditioning. Hot showers are wonderful—for that matter, so is not having to boil water before you drink it. And the not being shot at all the time. Huge bonus."

She leaned back toward him, uncomfortably close. "What about you?" she asked. "What do you think?"

"I guess I see the attraction. But—"

She put her hand on his thigh and squeezed hard, digging in her nails.

"First of all," she said, "don't go there. I know what you're about to start on about, and you know you shouldn't, not here. And even if you could, I wouldn't want to hear it. Just one night, okay? With no moralizing or guilt—just let me enjoy my damn drink, okay?"

A couple of people were looking at them now. Lena turned on her stool. "Are you all enjoying the show?" she asked.

They quickly turned away.

"I'm tired of this place," she said. "Let's find a different bar."

The next place looked pretty much exactly like the last.

They ordered a light meal and later had neon-colored ice cream, which he had to admit was very tasty. Then more drinks, and finally they walked around to the waterfront, which was as manicured as the rest of the city. A half-moon looked as if it was sailing in the harbor, and a few couples were rowing in iridescent flatboats.

They sat on a bench, and after a moment, he leaned over and embraced her. He felt her stiffen.

"What are you doing?" she demanded, pulling back.

"Settle down," he whispered. "Just pretend like we're kissing. I need to say something, and I don't want to be overheard."

She looked at him doubtfully, then leaned over so their cheeks were touching.

"Did you get a chip put in you?" he asked.

He felt her tense and then sort of sag.

"You followed me?" He wasn't sure how to read her tone. Was it despair, disappointment, or both?

"Yes," he said. "I'm sorry."

She began to quiver, and he realized she was crying.

"No," she said. "I brought a chip with me, a counterfeit one. So I could get in. So they can't hear you or see you, if that's what you're worried about. Not through me, anyway."

"Then why? Why go in there and not tell me about it?"

She drew back a little, so he could see her eyes, glistening in the city light.

"One last time," she whispered. "Once more, and I'll never ask this again. Amar—I need you to have faith in me."

He had been thinking about those words—and the last time she said them—for a long time.

"Okay," he said. "Okay." He stood up. "You should get some rest. You start the job tomorrow."

* * *

The next day Lena returned from work and flashed him the pass. She suggested they take a walk before dinner, so they took the lift down and were soon exploring one of the more bucolic areas of the city. Here the housing was grouped into little compounds with raised, shared green spaces, many of which were on the roofs of the houses.

"Terraces?" he asked.

"Yep," she said. "I grew up in that one." She pointed at one of three houses that shared both a terrace around them and a sort of courtyard between them.

"I thought you grew up in Gulf City," he said.

"Right," she allowed. "But in that model house. You could put a blindfold on me and I would be able to navigate the inside of it without much trouble."

"So this is the old home place," he said.

"As close as I'll ever get," she said. "So. Ask me how things went today."

"I saw the pass," he said. "I guess things went well."

"Yep. I'm now officially the quality control monitor for augmented processing units."

"Which means you do what?" he asked.

"Well, the units are inspected by automated assessors. The modules either pass or fail. If they pass, I send them to packing. If they fail, I direct them back to production."

"Couldn't the automated assessors do that?" he asked.

"Says the man whose job is to sit on a couch all day," she said with mock disdain.

"Don't get touchy," he said. "I'm not knocking your career."

"Just remember, I'm the one putting CORE on the table."

"How could I forget?" he sighed. Then he grew a little more serious. "How, um, *safe* do you feel there?"

"Very," she said. "The security system is top-notch. I was warned there are a few glitches in it, but those will be gone soon enough."

"And your boss? How is he?"

"I didn't meet the boss," she replied. "At least I don't think so. And my orientation was mercifully brief."

"So you think things are going to work out?"

She nodded. "I think it'll work out just fine," she said. Then she noticed he had stopped to stare at something. It was a little park, but unlike the others they had passed, it had some odd structures in it—tubes, narrow inclined smooth surfaces. Children were climbing and sliding on them. Others were swinging back and forth in flexible strips of plastic suspended from a metal frame by cables.

"Amar?"

"What is that?" he asked.

She laughed. "You're kidding, right?" She put her hand up to her mouth. "Oh god, you aren't kidding. It's a playground."

He knew each word individually, but the two together sounded weird.

"You didn't have playgrounds?" she asked in a

disbelieving tone. "You didn't play?"

"Sure, we played," Amar said. "We just didn't have a particular place for it. Or . . . things."

"You mean slides and swings and monkey bars?"

"We had monkeys," he said. "But they weren't drinkers."

"Funny," she said.

"My uncle made us this sort of thing to jump on once, from a tarp and some springs—"

"Like a trampoline."

"That was what he called it," Amar said. "ADVENT troopers trashed it the next time they came through."

"I guess that explains why you didn't have playgrounds," she said.

"There you go," he said as he continued to watch the children. "It doesn't seem like such a bad idea, a playground. Maybe one day . . ." He didn't finish the thought. He had been and was involved in the creation of several things— the Avenger and the Skyranger, for example. If he lived long enough, he would likely be involved in the building of any number of weapons, facilities, and defensive capabilities. But the odds that he would ever be in the place or have the time to build a playground seemed pretty close to nil. That would be for someone else to do, when it was all over. If it was ever going to be over.

"Yes," Lena said. "One day."

They began walking again, back toward the apartment.

"We were both drunk last night," she said. "Is there anything you want to say now that we're sober?"

"No," he said, "I think I covered it."

"Okay," she said. "Tomorrow."

"Tomorrow," he echoed.

CHAPTER 19

IT WAS THE sitting on his thumbs that was the most difficult part for Amar. Lena had been trained to recognize the particular "augmented processor" they needed for the Avenger, so it made perfect sense that she was the one tasked to work in the factory. But it left him too much alone with his thoughts. He could not stomach watching the media screen for more than a few minutes at a time—even the games available were so clogged with nonsense and outright lies that he couldn't bring himself to play them.

So he was left with his own thoughts, and right in the middle of that was his decision to trust Lena, a decision he second-guessed on a nearly hourly basis. But he also kept returning to the reason he was able to keep his resolution: He would be able to cancel the mission almost until the last second. If he did, he would probably die and would certainly never escape New Singapore. But no one else would be involved. Shen could try again with someone else, possibly in New Seattle, one of the other targets they had considered.

But he didn't believe Lena would lead him into a trap. He couldn't.

He continued to explore the city, thinking he could at least come to understand it better. The playground had been an eye-opener, a sign that he had his own prejudices and blind spots when it came to places like this. He still did not at all approve of New Singapore, but he felt he needed to understand it. The battle they were fighting against the ADVENT was not and could not be merely military. They needed the help of the people in the New Cities to win; they needed those people to *want* to be free. And right now, the ADVENT were winning the propaganda war.

As in New Kochi, the billboards here were much larger than those forced on the settlers, and they were constantly filled with images and stories of how the dissident few were making life harder for everyone, how twenty years of mutual cooperation for the common good of humanity and their benefactors were threatened by malcontent thugs who thought only of their own selfish needs. Even the contagion was being blamed on the resistance: The story was that it was a biochemical weapon developed by unscrupulous scientists to blackmail population centers, and that it had somehow gotten out of control.

And people bought it. He watched and listened to them in coffee shops, bars, and public squares.

On the other side of it, images of ADVENT peacekeepers were everywhere, posed heroically. Children wore ADVENT T-shirts and played Peacekeepers and Bad Guys, and no kid he saw ever wanted to be the Bad Guy.

He wondered, if he hadn't grown up where he had, if he didn't know the things he knew—would he be happy here? Would he watch his screen and eat CORE burgers and never wonder too much about what was really going on, why the aliens would try so hard to make people feel secure and happy, to draw them into the cities until there was no one left outside?

Maybe. Probably. But he didn't have the choice of accepting all of this without qualms, without wondering about the price.

* * *

The factory hummed along a constant twenty-four hours, so they went in at night. With Lena's pass and the "glitches" in security she had learned about, it wasn't difficult to get into the place.

Nothing manufactured here had any direct military use—most of the components, in fact, went into building entertainment systems and the autopilots for cars, trains, and transports. The only real exception seemed to be the processors themselves. This had seemed odd to Amar, so he had remarked on it during their last walk.

"Oh," Lena said. "No, the part we're talking about isn't used in ships of any kind. It's mostly used in traffic grid guidance systems and to replace the processors in older satellites. We wouldn't have had any chance at all to get our hands on anything meant for a modern military or deep-space ship. Those places are incredibly well guarded."

"But that's exactly what you're trying to repair—a ship."

"Yes. A twenty-year-old ship. The aliens have made serious upgrades in the past couple of decades. From what we can tell, their computer technology has changed substantially. But the APs they build here are old technology, perfectly adequate for our purposes. It will probably take some tweaking, but the Shens are quite sure they can make it work."

"So the security is minimal," he said.

"Yes."

"Do you think you could just walk in, take it, and walk out?"

"Walk in, yes. Take it, yes. Walking out will be a problem. The security is low, not nonexistent."

Now they had done the walking in part and were on to the taking.

The human staff was negligible, and only a few of them looked up as Amar and Lena passed through the corridors and open fabrication rooms. None took any notice of the empty backpack on Amar's shoulder.

In truth, almost everything in the factory was done through automation, with alien overseers and a few human collaborators at the top to give them a public face when they needed one. Most of the jobs that didn't involve public relations were like Lena's—humans watching machines that could already watch themselves. After all, the aliens didn't have any particular interest in educating humans in their technology.

Amar had the impression that most jobs in the city barely met the criteria to be called that. His time in New

Singapore had sharpened his sense of what the New Cities were *for*.

The cities of the past had for the most part evolved from crossroads or ports or defensible places. They had economic and social reasons for existing, and if they grew larger than a village, there were a number of demographic forces that caused that to happen. The old cities had been places of production, of commerce, of innovation in the social, technological, and artistic senses.

The function of New Singapore wasn't anything of the sort. It was about control, pure and simple. It had the outward form of a city but nothing of the essence.

Lena had sorted through the various configurations available to select the augmented processor with the best possible fit for the Avenger's computer. She had marked it, packed it, and sent it down to the loading dock, which was what they were entering now. Dimly lit with dull red lights, it was about half empty. Bundles of parts sat on small trams. Across the room was a pair of massive doors.

"What's through there?" he asked.

"A hangar," she said. "And a junction with a rail line. Some things get loaded onto rail, some are flown out—a few things go by truck."

"Well, let's find it first," he said.

"I have my handy inventory stick," she said, taking out a slim rod. It glowed and scrolled a few glowing characters.

"Right over here," she said.

The cylindrical container wasn't quite half a meter in length and half again that in diameter.

"That's the one?" he asked.

She examined it again and nodded.

"So exactly when does the alarm go off?"

"Everything that comes in here gets counted and has a match code to whatever is supposed to pick it up. If this leaves any other way than through the loading doors, there are alarms. If it goes out the loading doors but gets put anywhere other than its appointed destination, alarms again."

He examined the doors. They were thick and heavy, and would reel up into the ceiling when opened.

"Can we open these?" he asked.

"I don't have the codes or even access to the controls," she said.

He didn't think a rocket launcher would punch through them, either. That was too bad. It would make things much easier. The front door, however, could probably easily be compromised.

"I guess the plan is we take it and run for the front door," he said, stuffing the processor into the backpack.

"I was really hoping the brilliant chief could come up with a better plan," she said.

He shrugged. "We could hang out here until they open the doors and start loading," he suggested.

"There will be ADVENT security for that," she pointed out.

"Then I like my first plan," he said. "Give me a moment."

He paused only a moment before flipping on the radio.

* * *

As predicted, the alarm started braying as soon as they exited the dock. Amar had debated whether they should just walk and try not to draw attention, but he decided instead on running like hell. Lena hadn't reported any jabbers in the building in the four days she had been there, so the real danger was from the troops that would show up from the outside. The longer it took them to get to the front door, the greater the odds that they would meet with resistance.

This time they were noticed. Most of the workers were sort of milling in confusion, wondering why the alarm was sounding—until they saw Lena and Amar. Then they started ducking into rooms or under things. Whether they thought Lena and Amar *were* the danger or were running from the danger wasn't clear, but the billboards taught that where there were alarms and people running, there would soon be explosions and bullets.

One guy had a different reaction. He was a big man, tall and broad-shouldered, and he moved to intercept them, yelling for them to stop. Since he was blocking the corridor, there was no avoiding him.

Amar jabbed a fist at him, without slowing down.

"Do not!" he shouted. "You do not want to do that."

But the guy stood his ground.

Amar stopped just long enough to hand the backpack with the part to Lena.

"I don't know what you've stolen," the man said. "And I don't care. Just wait here until the police arrive."

"What's your name?" Amar demanded.

"Brian," the fellow said, looking mildly surprised.

"Brian, I'm in a hurry," Amar said. "You have exactly

two seconds to move out of the way."

"Now, look—"

Amar decided two seconds was too long. He feinted a punch to Brian's face; Brian threw up his hands to protect himself—also effectively blinding himself as Amar drove his hand into his solar plexus. Brian made a sucking sound; Amar swept his front foot and pushed him over while he was off-balance.

Big men could get away with a lot in a fight just by being big, which meant that a lot of them, especially civilians, thought it was *enough* to be big. Being big usually just stopped fights from happening to them, leaving them relatively . . . uneducated. If it had been Dux or Palepoi standing there, it would be Amar on the ground gasping for air, perhaps with a broken limb or two.

He let Lena keep the pack in case it happened again, and they continued on.

When they reached the front door, it was locked, naturally—the entire building was sealed. Odds were there were already ADVENT police closing in on the building, so they didn't have long.

"Now," he heard Lena say. She took him by the arm and pulled him back, away from the door.

He was surprised. He hadn't realized she also had a radio.

Suddenly one of the workers appeared from nowhere, dashing toward the exit, a look of pure terror on his face.

"Hey, no!" Amar shouted, but the young man showed no signs of slowing down. So he did the only thing he could. He sprinted forward, tackling the guy below the waist, trying to roll aside before . . .

The door exploded, along with a significant fraction of the wall. The shock knocked him another four meters and hammered the breath out of him. Black spots threatened to blot out his vision entirely.

He crawled off the young man.

"Are you okay?" he gasped, hardy able to hear his own voice.

The man looked around, bewildered. "I think?" he said.

"Run the other way," Amar said. "Farther into the building. You tell anybody you see, stay away from here."

That was all he had time for, he knew. Lena was tugging at his arm, and together they ran out the door, where the Skyranger was waiting. Dux was firing his rocket launcher again at some target down the street. Nishimura and Chitto were laying down cover fire.

A mag round skipped off the pavement, and another screamed by near his head. Across the street he saw something immense coming out of the shadows. It was like something from a nightmare, a nightmare inspired by the folktales his Malaysian grandfather had told of him. He only had a glimpse of it, but it looked like a cobra the size of a man.

It couldn't be real. . . .

Then it was out of sight, behind the Skyranger, and he and Lena were climbing into the ship. ADVENT troops were closing in from every direction, and it was definitely time to go. Chitto and Nishimura fired once more each and jumped in as well. Dux was right behind them, but as Lily kicked in the under jets, something wrapped around

Dux's ankle and yanked him back. He yelped and grabbed at the door, dropping his weapon. Amar threw himself on the floor and grabbed his wrists, trying desperately to pull him back.

Dux wasn't looking at him, but at whatever had a hold of him. His eyes were wide with terror and disbelief, but as he turned to look back at Amar, his face hardened and became grim, angry.

Then something yanked him so hard that all of Amar's strength and determination amounted to nothing. An infant could have done as well.

And Dux was gone. The Skyranger lifted free.

"Wait," Nishimura shouted at Lily. "Dux! We have to go back for him."

As she started forward, mag rounds sang through the open door and punched through the hull.

Amar realized everyone was looking at him, including Lily. His throat almost seized up. Nishimura started toward the door again, but he stopped her with his hand.

"Close it," he told Lily. "Get us out of here."

The Skyranger turned and accelerated toward the sky. The rattle of the weapons' fire was like popcorn popping, and like popcorn it diminished, the seconds between each concussion drawing further apart, until the only noise was the roar of the engines.

Amar regarded Nishimura. "Alejandra—" he began.

"No, Chief," she said. Her eyes were red. She had her helmet in her hands, resting on her lap. "You were right. I just lost it."

"That wasn't 'losing it,'" he said. "I would rather be in

a squad that cared too much about me than too little. But it was just too late."

He thought he was saying the words just to comfort her, but the minute they came out of this mouth he realized he meant it. He couldn't have said that a few months ago.

Nishimura put her head down. "I just hope he went in style. Took another couple with him. He would have wanted that."

"He bought us a working Avenger," Lily said. "That's not nothing."

New Singapore dropped away behind them. Somewhere, ADVENT was probably scrambling gunboats to come after them. They still might not make it home.

He turned his attention to Lena, whose gaze was fastened on the receding city.

"Are you all right?" he asked her.

She turned to him and nodded. "Thank you," she said.

"For what?"

"You know what," she said, and took his hand. After a few seconds, he gripped it back.

CHAPTER 20

AMAR WAS A little amazed at how much the Avenger had changed in the month or so since he had seen her. Not so much on the outside as on the inside. The first big surprise was that a hangar had already been cleared to house the Skyranger. It also contained the armory. Crew quarters fit for human beings had been constructed, and the tent city outside was vanishing as people moved into the ship.

A bar and restaurant similar to the Rathskeller on the Elpis was up and functioning. A workshop and an engineering department had been built. Most of this had been done using decades-old technology, although some of it was powered using Elerium. The result was something that felt a lot more like home—a human environment in an alien skin.

The "Enigma" chamber remained inaccessible, although it was unclear why. The elder Dr. Shen believed that once the power and computer systems were functioning, it would cease to be an issue.

Some individual systems were already online, including life support, which circulated breathable, climate-controlled atmosphere throughout the vessel. Others had been added; a jamming field had been erected around the ship—if a patrol did find them, the field should be capable of preventing communications from the immediate area, giving them a chance to deal with the enemy and keep their location secret for at least a little longer.

"We're a long way from flying, however," Dr. Shen told them. "Even after the computer is online, there are a number of parts we will have to either steal or fabricate."

He studied the item Amar and Lena had taken from New Singapore. It was a cylinder, flared slightly on both ends. Its metallic surface had a rainbow sheen, like titanium—except that the rainbow was always gradually shifting, like oil on water that something stirred now and then.

"This, however," Shen went on, "should work. I commend you all. I'm very sorry for the man you lost."

"Thank you, sir," Amar said.

"Well," Dr. Shen said, "let's see what we can do with this."

* * *

The rains of the northeast monsoon were tailing off, and the weather was growing drier and cooler, making patrols and hikes to the watchtowers much more pleasant. Amar held a briefing on the contagion and instructed patrols on how to identify it.

And things moved on. Lena was furiously busy the first few days after their return, but they both rose each morning before sunlight and shared a cup of coffee together. It wasn't as good as the stuff in New Singapore or even the pot Captain Simmons had brewed, but it didn't matter. The coffee wasn't really the point.

"When will you guys install the processor?" Amar asked on one such morning.

"We already have," she said. "We're taking baby steps in terms of connecting it to the rest of the systems, in case we find something ugly. Or something else ugly, I should say. We've already disabled several internal defense systems. We want to be pretty sure what we're turning on before we do it."

"That makes sense," he said. But it made him itchy. There was only so long that they could sit here, grounded, using energy, bringing in supplies, before being noticed. Caution was all well and good, but there were mounting risk factors in moving too slowly as well.

But there was no point in saying that. She knew it as well as he did.

They listened as the cloud forest changed its score from night to day, and the sky brightened.

"This is my favorite time of day," she said softly.

"Mine, too," he replied.

"I wish it lasted longer."

He took a little breath and let it out. "I'd like for it to last a lot longer," he said.

She peered at him over the brim of her coffee cup, sitting with her legs drawn up under her, looking beautiful in her ragged green fatigues and brown T-shirt.

"What?" she said. "Like all day?"

"Like from now on," he replied.

She pursed her lips and seemed about to say something, so he knew he had to get ahead of her.

"I love you," he said. "I was an idiot not to tell you before. I know I screwed things up. I know there aren't always second chances. But—"

"Hush," she said. "Just . . ." A brittle little smile appeared on her face. She couldn't quite meet his eyes.

She set the coffee cup down. "The reason . . ." she began, "the reason I went to the gene therapy center was because I suspected something, and I had to know if I was right."

"You don't have to tell me anything," he said. "I think we've been through this."

"I believe I do need to tell you," she replied. "You deserve to know."

He suddenly really didn't want to know, but he didn't say so. He just nodded and waited for her to gather herself and find whatever words she was looking for.

"My cancer is back," she said.

He heard the words, but he couldn't quite sort them out.

"You said gene therapy had cured it," he finally managed.

"It had," she sighed. "It did. I don't know what went wrong. For all I know, it's designed that way—if you stop the treatments it comes back, so you never want to leave the city." She shrugged. "I was starting to feel sick, like before. So when we were in New Singapore, I went in for a diagnostic."

"Okay," Amar breathed. "And you had it treated."

"No," she said. "No, I didn't."

"Why?" he asked. "We were *there*, you were in, and you had the fake chip. It would have been easy."

Her smile was a little more genuine this time. "Would you have, if it had been you?"

"I don't know!" he exploded. "I'm not sick. I haven't been sick. I've never thought about it."

"Let's just skip all of that soul-searching," she said. "You, Amar Tan, would not go into a gene therapy center to save your life. And neither will I. It was dangerous enough to get the checkup, but if they had done the therapy, they might have discovered my genome is already in the system. But even if that weren't a problem . . ." She ran her fingers through her hair.

"So that night, at the bar . . ." he said.

"Yeah," she said. "I knew I was sick, and I didn't want to think about it. I wanted to enjoy myself. Yes, I miss a lot of things about living in the city. But I know I can never really go back there."

Amar felt himself becoming increasingly more desperate, but he tried to keep his tone level, to not show it.

"Look," he said. "We can go anywhere—New Madrid, New Providence, any city—and act like we're coming in from the cold, just like we did before. You get cured; we leave. It's that simple."

"No," she said, "it isn't. We're lucky we got out last time, and someone died so we could do it. And that was for something important."

"Your life is important," he said.

"Amar, please understand. I'm not dead. I still have my life," she said. "For the first time, I really have my life. I don't know for how much longer, but however long it is, I want to spend it doing something important. Something my sister would have been proud of." She looked at him directly. "Something you would be proud of."

He was having a hard time forming words.

"Of course I'm proud of you," he finally got out.

"I was avoiding this conversation," she said. "I was hoping you wouldn't . . ." His throat caught. "Ah, wouldn't tell me what you just did. But now that you have . . ."

"Wait. You knew I was in love with you?"

"Of course, dumbass," she said.

He stared at her for a moment, stunned.

"Oh," he said at last. "But you don't—"

"Of course I do," she said. "God, you really are a numbskull."

"I'm starting to get that," he said.

"Yeah. *Starting* to." She wiped the corners of her eyes with her palms and picked her coffee back up. He watched her, tried to see every detail, the golden stars in her green eyes, the small spray of freckles on her forehead.

"What are you thinking?" she asked.

"I'm thinking . . ." he said. "I'm thinking you say you don't know how much longer you'll live. I don't know how long I've got either. Rider, Thomas, Toby, Dux—and a bunch before them—all gone in the blink of an eye. DeLao and Nishimura are the only people around who I've known for longer than a year. Odds are, next mission it'll be me. So I wish . . . whatever time we have left . . . I wish we could spend it together."

She reached for his hand.

"I can deal with that if you can," she said.

They were married the next day. They honeymooned farther up in the Ghats, where the air was cooler and thinner, and the Milky Way blazed like a white river in the sky.

* * *

The bridge of the Avenger was still a work in progress, but it was coming together. The ship's original sensors and some new ones engineering had built channeled and displayed information from the small—the temperature and humidity outside, for instance—to the grand, such as a relay that sorted thousands of coded radio transmissions by subject and priority.

By the way Sam was grinning, Amar figured there must be something else he'd been called up to see. He watched the analyst fiddle with some controls, and then took an involuntary step back as a column of blue light suddenly appeared in the middle of the room. Floating in the light was an image of Earth.

"Wow," he said.

"This is the hologlobe," Sam said. "Since we got the computer up and running, we've been able to do all sorts of cool things. This is one of them. We've wired in Vahlen's old network and started adding our own tracking information. We've now officially got a command center for our operations."

"That's pretty cool," Amar had to admit.

"I finally feel like I'm home," Sam gushed on. "Exactly where I need to be. It's all coming together, KB. You had a lot to do with that. You and . . . the others."

Amar didn't have to ask who he meant by "the others." The list was long, and growing longer.

"When we first met," Amar said, "you told us that you had found something worthy of their sacrifice. Do you still believe that?"

"Even I had my doubts at times," Sam admitted. "There were some pretty low moments, weren't there? But I promise you, it's going to pay off. We'll be able to organize on a scale we could only dream of before. The computer is working now. We've got a way to strategize at the global level. Once we figure out how to get this thing off the ground—"

"Yeah," Amar said. "That tiny detail."

"We've been trying to find Vahlen," Sam said. "We desperately need someone of her caliber in research. But no luck so far. She's like a ghost."

Amar thought it was likely she was quite literally a ghost, at least if you believed in such things. So many miles of open ocean, with days of sailing to reach anywhere. ADVENT patrols had managed to find his tiny boat. Vahlen would have been in either a relatively large ship or a fleet of little ones. Unless. . .

Unless the Elpis had a sister.

The thought made him smile, but he dismissed the speculation as pointless. Vahlen either couldn't be found, wasn't around to be found—or didn't want to be found. In any case, she wasn't going to be on the team.

Sam was still talking. "Anyway," he said, "there are other candidates for a chief research scientist, good ones. We should have one soon."

"When you pick one out, we'll go get them," Amar said. "But thanks for showing me this. I'd like to catch up on the defensive systems later, but right now I've got a lunch date with my wife."

On his way to the bar he passed Dr. Shen in the hallway. He was fiddling with a computer pad and looked perturbed.

"I just saw the hologlobe," Amar told him. "Congratulations."

"Thank you," the old man said distractedly. "I'm sorry, Amar, no time to talk."

"I understand," Amar said.

Lena wasn't in the bar, when he got there. He thought about going down to engineering to collect her, but if she was late, she usually had good reason to be.

So he sat alone. A few tables over, Nishimura was having an animated conversation with a new recruit. DeLao was at the bar, flirting with the bartender, a young woman from France whose other job was assistant mechanic on the Skyranger.

Chitto walked in, saw him, and came over.

"Got a minute, Chief?" she asked.

"Sure," he said. "Have a seat."

She looked around the bar. "Lot of new faces, huh?" she said.

"I was just noticing that," he said. There were now more

people in the Avenger whose names he didn't know than ones he did.

"They look so damn young," she said.

He laughed. "I was thinking that, too," he told her. "How old are you, Chitto?"

"Twenty-four," she said.

"Yeah," he said. "Nishimura, she's thirty. DeLao is around twenty-eight. I'm a year older than you. But we look like old-timers compared to some of these kids."

"It's all in the clean living, I guess," she said.

"It wasn't all that long ago that you were the rookie," he said. "I thought you looked like a baby."

"I know I was pretty green," she said. "I know you hated being stuck with me. But you hung in there for me, Chief. I appreciate that."

"So what's on your mind?" he asked.

She eyed him as if he was a little slow. "I just told you, Chief," she said.

"That's it?"

"It was big deal to me," she said. "I just never felt like it was the right time to thank you. We were always in the middle of something, or you were busy with other things."

"Oh," he said. "I was worried you were working up to quitting or something."

"Nah," she said. "I don't really have any other skills."

"Good," he said, "because I've been thinking. DeLao already has his own squad. I offered Nishimura a command, but she turned it down. I've been thinking you could head up a recon unit. What do you think?"

Her eyebrows lifted fractionally. He remembered when

Thomas had had this same conversation with him, what seemed like years ago.

"I think I'm not the leader type, Chief," she said. "It was hard enough to learn to be in a unit. You may remember I kind of tended to do things my own way."

"Believe it or not," he said, "that's a leadership quality. You might surprise yourself."

Oddly, she did look surprised. Very surprised, so much so that he thought she was having him on.

"Okay," Amar said. "You don't have to be sarcastic."

"No, Chief," Chitto said. "Listen."

He heard it then, close to inaudible at first, but growing steadily in volume.

CHAPTER 21

AT FIRST HE thought it was just some strange music someone had slipped into the intercom, some form of electronica.

But then he realized it sounded more like talking, a stream-of-consciousness soliloquy without breaks to draw breath. The words were unfamiliar and the articulation was very weird. Some of the sounds he was pretty sure the human voice couldn't reproduce. And it got louder and louder.

He didn't know what it was, but it sounded *wrong*—yet somehow familiar.

Now conversation had tailed off completely—everyone in the bar was listening. Most had puzzled expressions on their faces, but Nishimura looked horrified. She covered her ears and starting muttering in Spanish, and with creeping dread he began to understand why. Something about the cadence of the language, the tonal inflection, reminded him of the thing back in New Kochi, the monster that had reached into his brain.

And also of the jabbers—the language they spoke.

Trying not to lose it, he tapped on his radio. "Sam?" he said. "Sam? Dr. Shen?"

He got back only static.

"What the hell is it?" DeLao shouted. "Whoever is doing that—"

Amar had a bad feeling, and it was quickly getting worse.

"Chitto, Nishimura," he said, "find Palepoi and gear up. DeLao, get your squad together."

"What's happening, Chief?" Chitto asked.

"I have no idea," he said, "but it can't be good. Call everyone in. I want a squad guarding the bridge, one in engineering, one in the workshop, and one in the armory guarding the Skyranger. Nishimura, check in with the perimeter; make sure nothing is coming in. I'm headed down to engineering. My squad, come as soon as you're armed and armored, and someone drag my stuff down, please."

* * *

Engineering was a madhouse. Lily Shen was barking orders, and her half-panicked staff was scurrying around like confused ants.

"What's happening?" Amar demanded.

Lily looked up. Her expression was somewhere between irritated and panicked.

"The computer," she said. "Something's taking control of it."

"Something?"

"Lena, explain to him," she snapped. "I don't have time."

Lena looked at him apologetically. "She's freaking out," she said. "I don't blame her. The bridge has been sealed off, and her father is in there. Our internal communications have been shut down."

"What do you mean, 'sealed off'?" he asked.

"It's a security feature," she said. "In case the ship is invaded."

"I've already sent a squad there," he said, trying to sound calm. "I should hear from them soon. Lily said something had taken control of the computer. What exactly did she mean by that?"

"At first we thought it was a bug in the system," she said. "A virus or something. But now it looks like it's some kind of artificial intelligence."

"I don't understand," he said. "The computer has been on for weeks."

"But not fully operational," she said. "We tested it a bit at a time, remember?"

"Well, what happened?" he demanded.

"Obviously we missed something," she said. "As careful as we were, we weren't careful enough. The system is too alien. It must have been slightly aware the whole time, hiding, playing along with us, waiting for this moment."

"Bloody hell," he murmured.

"Yeah," she said. He could tell she was worried, but she shot him a little smile.

"You're really cute when you say that, you know," she said.

"You mean sexy," he said.

"That's exactly what I meant." She kissed him. "Go do your job," she said. "I have to get back to mine."

* * *

Nishimura, Chitto, and Palepoi showed up a few minutes later. Amar took his gear from Chitto and began putting it on.

"DeLao," he called. "What about the bridge?"

"Locked down, Chief," he replied. "Can't get it open. There's a kid here from engineering working on it, but so far, no luck."

It was getting hard to hear, as the ghastly chatter rose to a nearly deafening level.

And then, very suddenly, it stopped. Dead silence followed for the space of a few heartbeats.

"*Zao gao!*" Lily swore into the stillness.

Amar stood frozen, waiting—for what he wasn't sure.

Then the lights went out, and they were in utter darkness. Lily uttered a few more colorful Mandarin phrases, and several people screamed. Amar flipped on his helmet light.

"Everyone keep calm," he bellowed.

Then the diesel generator kicked in, and the auxiliary lights came on. He made his way to Lily.

"What's happening?" he asked.

"I'm frozen out," Lily whispered. "It's completely taken over the ship. And it has turned off the air."

"And sealed all of the hatches, I would assume," Amar said.

"Of course," she replied. He saw that she was trembling.

"You've got this," he told her. "You can do it."

She looked at him. "The noises," she said. "Did you hear?"

"Yes," he said. "I get it. But you have to shake it off and save us, right?"

She took a deep breath. "Of course," she said.

"Okay," he said. "So how long have we got? Before we suffocate?"

"That's difficult to calculate," she said. "We have at least a few hours before carbon dioxide levels start to become toxic." She thought for a moment. "If I can devise some way of scrubbing the CO_2, we could last a little longer."

"How about this?" he asked. "Is there some way to manually open any of the outer hatches?"

"No. Not without explosives, and maybe not even then," she said.

"Chief?" That was DeLao, over the radio.

"Yes, go ahead."

"The bridge just opened up," he said.

"Is Dr. Shen okay?" he asked.

"Yes, he and Sam are fine," DeLao said.

Amar turned to Lily. "Why would the AI lock the bridge and then unlock it?"

"I don't know," she said. "It doesn't make any sense." Her brows beetled up. "Unless—"

"Guys," Lena interrupted. "Lily, Amar—look at this."

He stepped over to see what she was studying so intently. It turned out to be a screen divided up between security cameras they had installed early in the refit process. At first he didn't see what had attracted Lena's attention.

"Here," she said, pointing. "That's the Enigma chamber."

"Oh," Amar said.

Slowly, as he watched, the hatch began to open.

"Unless the computer didn't lock the bridge," Lily continued. "Maybe the security system locked it before the AI got control of it."

"Oh, no," Lena said.

Amar keyed the radio. "Everyone, watch for hostiles, originating in the lower fore of the ship. Repeat, we may have hostiles."

His earpiece crackled.

"ADVENT?" DeLao asked.

"I don't think so," Amar said. "But it could be just about anything else. Watch the lifts and the access stairs and squeal if you need help. If they get through you, they can come at us from any number of directions. Akira, same for you guys in the workroom. We have to keep these things on the lower deck."

"Right, Chief," Akira said.

"Mak, are you there?" Amar asked.

"Mak" was Mukharymova, a fresh recruit from the New Moscow area, but she was anything but green, having fought with an isolated cell since the age of fifteen. She had dark eyes and honey-touched hair that was driving half of the men crazy, but if she noticed the attention, she ignored it. Her squad was still in the armory.

"Yes sir," she replied.

"Get down here and guard engineering. We're headed to the Enigma chamber."

He signed off. "Come on," he said.

The Avenger, he thought, suddenly didn't feel like home at all.

The armory was on the top deck of the ship, in the rear. The Enigma chamber was in the front of the craft and three decks down, on the same level as engineering, which was in the back, underneath the bar and the armory. Between engineering and the Enigma chamber were three interconnected compartments that currently didn't have any use.

Through these they now advanced, cautiously opening each hatch until they came to the third, from which they could see the now-open Enigma chamber. Amar couldn't make out anything inside other than darkness and something in the distance radiating a pale green light.

He was about to give the order to move up when something came hurling through the hatch and bounced off the wall.

"Grenade!" he shouted, ducking back behind the bulkhead. Thunder boomed, and a blast of heat and fury came through the hatch.

Amar leaned around. He saw movement and fired without waiting to see what it was. His bullets rang like they were hitting a steel wall.

"Robots!" he yelped.

This particular robot was flying, and another came out just behind it. It looked a little like a human torso with no head and nothing from the waist down. It had one arm with a mechanical claw and the other was just a long tube.

Which suddenly spat green fire. Not a mag rifle, some

kind of energy, and *hot*. He felt the scorch of it in the air, even though it missed.

Nishimura shot the same one he had, and it went rattling back against the wall. Amar tossed in a grenade, seeing as he did so more robots streaming through the opening. And they had nowhere to go except through Amar and his squad. If he got pushed back, though, they could potentially go anywhere using the lifts or stairs connecting the decks.

For a while, they managed to hold them. A few made it through the door but were gunned down as soon as they did. A pile of robotic debris was beginning to build up in the chamber.

But finally, there were too many. One shot Palepoi, sending him stumbling back. Nishimura came up and sliced its weapon off, but another was right there. Amar shot it, threw another grenade, and gave the order to fall back to the next room just before it went off. He slammed the hatch, but it wouldn't lock.

Palepoi, still on his feet, fired another rocket as the hatch popped back open. Then they set up and waited for the assault to continue. They had now been pushed back almost to Mak's position.

"DeLao," Amar said, "report."

"Nothing yet, but we can hear you guys catching hell. What is it?"

"Mechanicals," Amar said. "Figures. What else could last twenty years in a sealed chamber?"

It was starting to feel hot and stuffy. The scent of propellant and ozone clogged the air. Was he imagining it, or was it already getting hard to breathe?

Nishimura leaned out and fired.

Amar glanced over at Palepoi and nodded at him.

"I'm okay, Chief," he said. "Just a little scorched. If that had been a mag, I'd be done."

"Okay, Chitto, go back and set up a supply line. We need people to walk ammo down from the armory. Tell Mak to move someone up to take your place."

"Rather stay here, Chief," she said.

"Not much use for a sniper in this situation," he pointed out.

"Fair," she said. He and Nishimura covered her retreat.

"KB," the radio said, "this is Sam."

"What's up?" Amar asked.

"I think I can take control of the ship," he said. "Dr. Shen says there's a kill switch—"

"Hell yes," Amar said. "Do it."

"I'm on my way," Sam replied. "I just wanted to keep you in the loop."

"Thanks," Amar said. "Do it."

Things were looking up. The robots kept coming, but with two squads working together and a steady supply of ammunition, they weren't making any advances. They seemed to have them contained and were even starting to push them back.

He realized he hadn't heard from Sam in a while, so he tried the radio. The analyst didn't answer.

"DeLao?"

But he didn't answer, either.

"Has anyone heard from DeLao?"

"Haven't heard anything, Chief," Akira said. He was in the workroom, a compartment below the bridge. "It's real quiet up here. Should I send someone up?"

"No," he said. "Keep your position. Engineering?"

"This is Lily Shen," his earpiece informed him. "What has happened to my father?"

"I don't know," he said. "I'm going to find out. Could just be a problem with the radio." He didn't believe that, but he needed to give her something to hang on to.

"Sam said something about a kill switch," he said. "Where is that?"

"There is an access tube that runs between the hull and the bridge," she said. "There are a series of kill switches Dad placed there in case something like this happened. They should literally cut the computer off from the rest of the ship, at which point we can open the hatches using the generator. I should have been able to detonate them from here, but something has severed the connection—perhaps the computer itself, using some sort of remote. Sam went to try and execute manually."

But Sam wasn't answering the radio.

"I'm coming back," he said. "Show me."

Gunfire rattled behind him as he came back into engineering. Lily had pulled up a detailed plan of ship. He studied it for a few minutes.

"What do we do when we get there?" he asked.

"Don't worry," Lena said. "I'm going along. I know the procedure, and there's no time to teach it to you."

CHAPTER 22

THE SOUND OF gunfire intensified behind them as Amar and Lena made their way up the stairs with Palepoi and Nishimura.

Amar paused. "What's going on down there, Mak?" he asked.

"Chief," his earpiece said. "Mak here. I think we may have gotten the last of them. We're proceeding into the Enigma chamber."

"Don't fall asleep, Mak," he cautioned. "You don't know what's in there."

On the way up, they paused to look in on Akira and his bunch, who seemed almost bored.

Mak came back just as they reached the top level.

"Nothing moving in here, Chief," she said. "I think we got them all." There was pause. "Weird," the Russian said. "These look sort of like coffins."

Amar peered around the corner. He was now looking

down the passage that the bridge opened from, where DeLao's squad was supposed to be.

But the corridor was empty. And the hatch to the bridge was closed.

Someone on the radio link started screaming.

"Mak?" Amar said.

"Chief—" the Russian gasped.

Then nothing, as if her radio had been destroyed. But below, the sound of gunfire began again.

What the hell is happening, he wondered, fighting a sudden, almost overwhelming sense of dread.

Coffins. He remembered Vahlen's lab, the alien-human hybrid in cryosleep. . . .

One thing at a time, he told himself sternly. Do the job in front of you. Trust the other squad leaders to do theirs.

"Where is the access corridor?" he asked Lena.

"Down past the bridge," she said.

"Okay," he said. "The two of us are going down there. Nishimura, Palepoi—cover us."

As they crept down the passage, Amar roved his gaze everywhere, but he paid special attention to the bridge hatch, afraid that it was going to suddenly spring open.

But they passed it uneventfully and reached the stairs.

Then the bridge door opened, and DeLao stepped out. He aimed his rifle at Amar and pulled the trigger.

Amar was already moving, pushing Lena into the stairwell. Two bullets smacked into his armor on his left side and nearly spun him around. He managed to stagger through the hatch before DeLao could shoot him again.

"Amar—" Lena began.

"Just go," he said. "Do it."

His ribs felt like a cinderblock had been slammed into them, and he was sure some of them were broken, but there wasn't any blood.

He leaned out for a look. DeLao was waiting, and now Amar noticed what he hadn't before, at least not on a conscious level.

DeLao's eyes. Empty, glowing, like Nishimura's back in New Kochi.

Bullets thudded into the bulkhead as he drew back again, but not before seeing something else coming out of the hatch, something not human at all.

"Chief?" Nishimura said.

"Try not to kill DeLao if you can help it," he said. "But don't let anything get to the stairs."

Then he started up after Lena as the fireworks began in the corridor.

The narrow stairs took him up past the crew quarters and an unassigned room above them. Beyond that they continued until they reached a long horizontal shaft lit by cool blue light.

Lena was waiting for him. She shot him in the stomach as soon as he stepped into the corridor.

He gasped and staggered back. His legs suddenly felt like rubber, but oddly there was no pain, just the sense of impact. Behind her, he saw a misshapen shadow and huge phosphorescent eyes.

"Lena," he pleaded. "Don't. Fight it. I love you."

She took a step forward and aimed at his face. He saw her hand was trembling. Her trigger finger twitched, once, twice.

Amar rolled over so he had a clear shot at the thing and then sprayed it with bullets. It staggered back a meter and then started forward again, screeching. Amar took aim at its huge, onion-shaped head and blew it into fragments.

Lena shrieked and dropped the gun. Amar staggered up and took her in his arms.

"I know," he said, brushing her hair with his palm. "I know."

"I shot you!" she cried. "Oh my god, Amar—I shot you."

"Lena," he said. "Listen. I'll be okay. You have to focus. The kill switches. I have to watch the stairwell. It's okay."

It wasn't, of course. His gut was burning now, and his body felt unreal. He knew he was on the verge of blacking out.

"You can do it," he said. "You have to do it."

She pulled back from him. Her face was streaked with tears, but he recognized the look of determination on it.

"Okay," she said. She started down the corridor.

"I'll watch your back," he said.

"Probably better if you watch the stairs," she said. It took him a few beats to realize she was trying to make a joke.

She went a few meters and then crouched down. "Crap," she said.

"What?" he grunted.

"It's Sam," she called back. "He's dead."

Of course he was. Amar was trying to picture what had happened. The Sectoids had unobtrusively moved up from below, taken control of DeLao and Sam, and probably some of the others. They had quietly killed everyone else, dragged them into the control room. . . .

He heard something coming up the stairs; he drew a

bead on the next landing and waited.

"The kill switches," Lena said. "They've been disabled."

Of course they had.

It came quicker than he thought it would. All limbs and horror, the Chryssalid almost seemed to fly up the stairs. He started firing as soon as he saw it, but it nearly made it all the way to him before finally succumbing. He watched it thrash back down toward the bottom.

"Chief," Nishimura said. "They're coming from everywhere. Swarming. Palepoi is down."

"Fall back," he said. "Defend engineering."

"But Chief—"

"Go," he said. "There's nothing you can do for us alone. I'm in a defensible position."

A streak of green plasma seared past his head, and down on the landing he saw another Sectoid scrambling toward him. It was smaller than the one he'd just killed and much smaller than the one in New Kochi.

It died more easily, too, but there were plenty more behind it.

He ducked back behind the wall to reload. Lena was right there.

"Give me your pistol," she said. "So I can help."

"I've got this," he said. "You need to figure out how to re-enable the kill switches."

"I can't do that," she said. "But there's another option, if you have a grenade left."

"You mean we can just blow it up?" he asked, then fired at the next monster as it started up toward them, forcing it back down.

"Sure," she said. "This is where the AI gets its power. The kill switches were designed to do that without, you know, destroying the whole area. But we don't have the luxury of being neat anymore."

"So we just toss the grenade down there?"

"I'd better place it," she said. "Can it be set for a delay?"

"Up to twenty seconds," he said.

"Okay," she said. "Stand up."

"I'm not sure I can," he said.

"You have to," she said. "Once I set the grenade, we're going to have to run like hell. We don't want to be up here when the power conduits rupture."

"That puts us running down into them," he said, taking another shot.

"Yep," she said. "So stand up and give me your pistol."

He wasn't sure where he found the strength, but using the wall as support, he managed to get back on his feet. She took his handgun and grenade and went back down the corridor.

And that was when the spider tried to get back into his skull.

He tried to focus on the pain, to beat it back. He staggered down a step, to find it, kill it before it could take control of him.

His legs betrayed him, and he stumbled and went crashing down the stairs. He hit the landing, agony digging in his every nerve as he fired blindly, and the spider walked out, but it wasn't dead—he could feel it, waiting. His vision was blurring; he made out vague shapes scrambling up toward him.

Lena was suddenly at his side. She pulled out his sidearm and fired across him, down the stairwell. Another one of the things gibbered in pain.

"Come on," she said. "We've got to go down there."

"We can't," he said.

"We have about six seconds," she said. She put her arm under him and heaved, and once more he gathered his feet under him.

Another one of the little monsters stuck its head around the next landing, and Lena put a hole in it. They managed to stumble down another flight.

Then everything went white, and something slapped him in the back, *hard*.

The next thing he saw was Lena in front of him, legs braced, firing his pistol at something he couldn't see. He started to rise up and saw three plasma bursts sleet through her unarmored body. She took a step forward, and they shot her again.

She fell back next to him. She looked at him and tried to say something, but his ears were ringing, and he couldn't make out the words.

He rolled off of his rifle and shot at the first thing he saw move, but everything was blurring now, and he couldn't find a target. Or move his hand or, finally, see at all.

But he could still hear, and what he heard sounded like gunfire, far off in the distance.

CHAPTER 23

IT SEEMED TO Amar that it had been dark for a long time, dark and deeply silent. If it was night, it was starless and long, as if the world had stopped turning.

Maybe, he thought, morning would never come again.

Part of him hoped it wouldn't.

But then, very faintly, the line of the horizon appeared, dividing first gray and black, then coral and indigo, saffron and azure, until finally—like the eye of a god opening—the edge of the sun appeared.

Again he wondered at how quickly it rose, how beautiful it was. He watched in awe as the golden path appeared on the waters and stretched out to his feet.

He wondered if he walked that path, where it would go, what things he would see. But before he set foot on it, he saw something coming toward him—small with distance, but growing larger by the moment.

A breeze lifted, and very faintly he heard something —
not quite music, but a cadence.

And words.

Tyger, Tyger, burning bright,
In the forests of the night;
What immortal hand or eye
Could frame thy fearful symmetry?

The words continued, and the tiger stopped in front of
him. For a very long moment, it held his gaze. He saw the
faint reflection of himself in the golden spheres of its eyes.
He felt its hot breath on his face.

Then it went around him and continued on across the
water.

Amar awoke on his back, staring at the ceiling. When he
turned, he saw that he was in the infirmary of the Avenger.
He had an IV drip in his arm.

Chitto was sitting in a chair next to him. She was just
closing a book.

"Hey, Chief," she said. "Glad you're back."

"Yeah," he said.

He remembered. At the end it was messy, but he
remembered. Yet he still had to ask.

Chitto told him what he needed to hear, and he nodded.

"Any other questions, Chief?"

"No," he said. "Not right now."

"That's okay, then," she said. "I was just going anyway."

He nodded at her book. "What's that you're reading?"
he asked.

"Oh, this?" she said. "It's just some poems by a guy named Blake."

"Where did you get a book all the way out here?"

She shrugged. "I've had it all along," she said. "Brought it with me from home."

Then she left.

* * *

Lily Shen came to see him later, but how much later he wasn't sure.

"I heard you were awake," she said.

"For what it's worth," Amar replied.

"It's worth a lot," Lily said. "To all of us. If it hadn't been for you —"

"That's . . . I don't want to hear that," Amar said. "Tell me what happened. Obviously we're still alive."

"The aliens were in cryosleep," Lily said. "The AI woke them up. They seem to have deployed the robots first, as a ruse, while the Sectoids infiltrated the bridge area. They took control of DeLao and one of his men, and they killed the other two. We found them on the bridge, along with my father."

"Your father . . ." he began.

"They didn't kill him," she said. "But they interrogated him." Her voice dropped. "It was too much for him," she said. "I don't think he will recover."

"I'm sorry to hear that," Amar said.

"We've all lost loved ones," she said. But he could see on her face and hear in her voice that she wasn't ready to lose him.

He closed his eyes. "So the grenade worked, I guess."

"Yes," Lily said. "The damage was pretty terrific; it will set us back a bit. But we survived. The mission survives. As does hope. Thanks to you and Lena, the AI is completely defanged."

"I've heard that before," Amar said.

She shook her head in the negative. "We got it right this time."

He hoped that was true. He had no interest in a do-over.

"And then Chitto," she said. "More than half of the soldiers were dead, but she somehow pulled together what was left and brought them up to support you. Killed the last of the aliens, rescued you and my father."

He felt an unexpected pulse of pride.

"Chitto?" he said. "She did that?"

"Yes, she did," Lily said.

"Did Nishimura survive?"

"Yes, she made it," Lily said. "She's off on a recruiting mission at the moment."

"How long have I been out of it?"

"Two weeks," she said. "They had to do some pretty complicated surgery on you, and they still weren't sure you were coming out of it—until you did." She smiled her distracted little smile, and he could tell her attention was no longer on him. She had things to do. He was surprised she had spent this long with him. She stood up. "Do you need anything?" she asked.

"No," he said.

Lily took a few steps and then turned back.

"She's a hero, KB," she said. "She saved us all. Even

with the aliens dead, we would still have suffocated."

"I know," Amar said.

* * *

He was in bed for another week before he could slowly, painfully, move around. Lily told him he should take some time off, but he knew that wouldn't do him any good—that he would just think about Lena, about all the time he had wasted before finally bending to his heart.

So he went back to work. There was plenty to do—recruits were flowing in from everywhere. They needed training, and assignments, and a little perspective.

By the time Nishimura returned, he was strong enough to have a beer with her. She was the last living member of his original squad. They toasted their fallen and told a few funny stories about each. It didn't feel good, exactly, but it did feel right.

"I brought up the new guy," she told him.

"Who is that?" He wanted to know.

"The new head of research, Tygan. Pretty sharp guy. He used to work in the gene therapy labs with ADVENT, but he got religion and defected to us."

"He must have been pretty convincing," Amar said. "The security risk involved in bringing somebody like that in . . ."

"We checked him out pretty good," she said. "Anyway, you know as well as I do that there are good people in the cities. They only need to know the truth. Some find it for themselves, and some have to be shown it."

He knew she was talking about Lena, but he wasn't

ready to talk about her. He might never be.

When Nishimura saw that he wasn't going to bite, she changed tack.

"What do you think our next mission will be?" she asked.

"No telling," he said.

But he was thinking something else—that maybe he didn't have another mission in him. That he had done his part, given all he could. That maybe it was time for him to go home, see if any of his cousins were alive, help them survive.

* * *

"We've done good work here," Dr. Shen said, a few days later. "I hope you all know that. I hope you take it to heart."

There wasn't much left of Doctor Raymond Shen. He was shockingly thin and dissipated. His arms quivered uncontrollably, and his speech was slurred.

He was sitting up in his bed, but it looked like he might topple over at any moment. Lily and a nurse stood on either side of him, ready to catch him if he did.

"Unfortunately," he said, "it doesn't appear likely that I will be here to see this ship fully operational, much less the end of what is going to be a long and wearying war. So I would like to discuss what comes next.

"My daughter is more than fit to replace me in engineering. We have our new head of research, so we need not worry about that. But for XCOM to move forward, it needs structure. It needs someone in charge."

He was silent for a moment; it looked as if just that much speaking had worn him out.

"There is a possibility," he said. "It is not yet confirmed. But if it is true, I can die knowing that I left all of this in good hands, that the human race has a fighting chance."

"What possibility, sir?" Amar asked.

"There is quite a bit you need to know," Dr. Shen said. "Things I've kept mostly to myself or shared only with Lily. But time's arrow has found me, and I can't be the sole repository of so much that is so critical."

He seemed to be having difficulty breathing, and for several long moments he tried to get more words out, without success.

"Dad—" Lily began, but he waved her off.

He closed his eyes, and when he opened them he was able to continue, in a wheezing, raspy ghost of a voice.

"The . . . setback . . . was unfortunate. I know the word is too mild," he said, looking apologetically at Amar. "We all lost so much. But you must promise me you will carry on."

In that moment, Amar's doubts dropped away. Lena had once told him he liked to make the easier choices when it came to his feelings. Staying with XCOM was going to be hard. He would be reminded of her every day. He would grow close to comrades and then lose them, too.

But he didn't want to forget her, and if his presence brought one more rookie out of the field alive, it would be worth it.

"I promise," he said.

Dr. Shen died three days later. They buried him in the cloud forest with Lena, DeLao, and all of the rest of the

Avenger's dead. Like them, his grave wasn't marked, but its position was recorded to the millimeter.

Because one day they would all have markers, and their names would be known, and history would remember how and when humanity turned the corner and began the fight to take back their planet—and their destiny.

In Flanders fields the poppies blow
Between the crosses, row on row,
That mark our place: and in the sky
The larks still bravely singing fly
Scarce heard amid the guns below.

We are the dead: Short days ago,
We lived, felt dawn, saw sunset glow,
Loved and were loved: and now we lie
In Flanders fields!

Take up our quarrel with the foe
To you, from failing hands, we throw
The torch: be yours to hold it high
If ye break faith with us who die,
We shall not sleep, though poppies grow
In Flanders fields

—JOHN MCCRAE

EPILOGUE

THE BOY LOOKED even younger dead, he thought. What was his name? Ivan?

Ivan. He and the rest had tried to sabotage a gene therapy clinic, as he heard it. Only two of them got out and made it to the settlement, and one was Ivan.

But the kid had taken a round and died a day later. He had learned about it when he went in for supplies.

He found the surviving kid digging Ivan's grave. The boy watched him as he arrived. He didn't look any older than sixteen. He had wide, expressive eyes that he should have been used to woo girls rather than to look through a rifle sight.

"What do you want?" the boy asked.

"Nothing," he said. "I just came to pay my respects."

"Oh," the boy said. "You knew him?"

"Not much," he replied. "But if you want some advice—

forget burying him. Get the hell out of here before a patrol finds you."

"He deserves a burial," the boy said.

"I bet he'd rather you stayed alive, if he had any say in the matter."

The boy straightened, and his eyes narrowed.

"You're him, aren't you? The guy Ivan came to see."

He just shrugged.

"Yes, it's you," the boy said. "Ivan kept going on about what a great man you were, how you could turn everything around, that all he had to do was talk to you. And what did you do? Showed him your back. Great man, my ass. So I've no use for you, *pendejo*—or your advice."

He spat and then went back to digging.

"That's fine with me, kid," he said.

He got his supplies and went back to his hidey hole. He turned on the radio and took a seat, setting a bottle of whiskey in front of him on his "table."

He hadn't listened to the radio for a long time—it was too depressing. But in the last few weeks—well, it seemed like something was starting to happen. Somebody was recruiting, and on a pretty decent scale. Battles were being won. Small victories, true, but victories nonetheless. But more than that, there was a sudden surge of what he could only call hope—and what's more, that hope seemed to have a name.

Avenger.

He unscrewed the cap of the whiskey bottle, thinking about Ivan, about the boy digging his grave who probably wouldn't make it to sundown.

Not his problem. Nothing to be done.

He lifted the bottle.

Then, with a heavy sigh, he set it back on the crate and screwed the cap back on. He went into his shack, found his shotgun, and checked to make sure it was loaded.

Something was happening out there, finally. It was time he found out what.

The boy looked up at him when he returned. He saw the shotgun and jumped for his rifle.

"Hang on, son," he said. "Just give me the shovel so we can get this done and get out of here."

The boy stared at him as if he was kidding, but when it sunk in that he wasn't, he handed him the shovel.

"When Ivan came to see me," he said, pushing the shovel into the dense soil, "he had someone he wanted me to see. Would you know who that was?"

"Yeah," he said. "I think so."

"When we're finished here, you'll take me there. Okay?"

"Yes," the boy said. "Yes, sir."

He kept digging.

"It's Bradford, right?" the boy said, after a moment. "Mr. Bradford?"

He leaned on the shovel and looked at the boy. "What's your name?"

"Arturo."

"Don't call me that, Arturo," he said. "That's not a name that needs to get around. Just call me Central."

They laid Ivan in the ground, went back to his place, and packed up what few possessions they would need. When the patrol found his shack, he and Arturo were long gone.

THE END

ACKNOWLEDGMENTS

I WOULD LIKE to thank Matt Knoles at 2K Games. To the Firaxis team—Peter Murray, Lindsay Riehl, Garth DeAngelis, Scott Wittbeker, Jacob Solomon, Chad Rocco, and Garrett Bittner—thanks for creating such an amazing universe and navigating me through it. At Insight Editions, thanks to Vanessa Lopez, Elaine Ou, Greg Solano, and Chrissy Kwasnik, and special thanks to my editor, Ramin Zahed.